DIEGO IS HERE

A NOVEL BY
GWEN DELP

This book is dedicated to my husband, Joe, and our shared history of growing up in the Yakima Valley. It is also dedicated to the garden I grew up in that was grown by my father, Kenny Puyear, a master of gardening. And then there is my wonderful mother, Virginia, who taught me all I know about flowers and cooking and loving your family.

Laurel

Beginnings and endings are not always clear. So many times, they are organized in our minds after the fact. Was that the beginning of the end? Is this the end of the beginning? Am I in the middle of this? How did this happen? Sometimes time gives clarity.

Laurel was unsure of just where she was in her knowing about herself. Maybe it was the end of the beginning and or maybe it was just the beginning. Had she known some things about herself for a long time and right now it was becoming clearer? Or was this something new and she really could call this the beginning? It just was not clear at this point. She was not even sure if it mattered.

Things were changing, that was a given. She was moving out of her apartment, and she was returning to her childhood home. Circumstances in the family had dictated this and there was really no question in her mind about whether it was the right thing to do.

She was leaving a job she did not truly love or possibly even like. It was her chosen field, hard won with an expensive education and loans hounding her every month. What made her chose Library Science? It was boring and her boss was a dinosaur. Yes, it was the Seattle Public Library but the work was dull and the salary not great. If this is what a master's degree from the University of Washington got her then she was sadly mistaken for pursuing it.

When she told her boss that she was leaving and moving back to her home in Eastern Washington, she gasped and said, "Laurel, why are you throwing away this opportunity? You are too intelligent to be stuck in some small-town library system." Her boss did not even ask her what she planned to do or why she was leaving. She just acted like it was a personal affront to her and she never asked anything else. That was it.

She had some good friends from her college years and some from work. When she told them they acted like she was going away to die in a remote part of the world. The thought of living in the heat in the summer and snow in the winter was just something they would not choose. They worried about the politics and what if you want to meet a man and who is there but rednecks and farmers. They argued that the cost of living is less, but the quality of life is terrible. What will you do on weekends? How can you give up an apartment that is right downtown?

She could give it up, no problem. The apartment was tiny. It was convenient to all the things she might want to do at any given time, but it was old, smelled musty and the windows were impossible to pry open. Her view was an alley with a dead tree and occasional homeless people shooting up. She did not have friends over because she had very little to sit on and she had been to their apartments. They had family money. Parents who purchased furniture whenever they flew into town. Parents who put an extra couple of thousand a month in their bank accounts, just in case. Some had married and two incomes helped a lot. No one had children yet.

She was not embarrassed by her apartment, so much as she felt it was her only place to just be the girl from a little town in a big city. It was shabby, like the house she grew up in. She did not feel sorry for that, just wanted to keep it for herself with no explanations needed. She never cared about the material trappings of being a "Seattle" woman.

Packing up took one afternoon. She basically took her clothes and a couple pictures. The kitchen was fully stocked with thrift store cracked dishes and odd silverware. She would not need it anymore. She put those things in a box and labeled it, "For the new tenant" and left it on the kitchen counter.

She did not have a car. She had sold hers a while ago and was happy to have no more parking tickets and garage fees. She rolled her suitcase down to the train station and left for Yakima on the 2:30 train.

Simon

He sat on the edge of his bed with the hard lumpy mattress and the creaking springs. He looked at the worn braided rug and the rough wooden floor beneath it. He hated this room. He hated this house. He did not live here anymore, but he was here to help Laurel.

He could hear his dad downstairs, coughing and moving some kind of furniture around. He really should go down and help him and make him stop exerting himself. But he found himself still sitting on the mattress and staring at the floor.

He could smell the dust in the room. Yakima Valley dust. Always present, always on every surface. Even the window sill had a nice little pile of dust that had seeped through the warp-ing boards. The window had wavy glass and he could see his car in the driveway, parked beside his father's old pickup. His car did not fit the scene. It was a small car, new and shiny, but getting layered with the dust from the driveway as he sat there. The fucking dust.

The orchard was in bloom right now. Apples and a lone apricot tree in the yard. That was something he missed. Fresh apples picked from the tree. Apricot jam jars filled to the brim in the cellar. In Bellingham, up north, he did not have dust, but he did not have an apricot tree in his yard. Instead, he had a deck on a condo, overlooking the Bay. His bike and his lone lawn chair occupying the deck and usually a dead plant he had moved from the house so he could stop looking at it.

He already, in one day, missed the smell of the sea and the ever-changing colors of the bay. But home called and here he was du-tifully trying to be a good son. But he would never be as good as Laurel. Never ever in the eyes of his dad.

His mom, now that had been a different story. She too hated dust. She wanted the sea. She wanted the rain and the green assaulting you each time you turned a corner. She under-stood getting away and she remained trapped until recently, when she just died. Quickly, without warning, and without a goodbye. Just gone and that was it.

When Simon arrived the only thing his father said to him was, "You will need to stay until your sister Laurel gets settled. Well, and of course, until after the funeral. I need some help around here, so don't go running off."

Running off? Where in the hell did he think Simon was going to go? He no longer associated with anyone from his childhood. It had been painful enough to share it with the people he knew as a kid. He did not fit into the scenario that was his childhood. He was always "different", and everyone let him know that. It was not a reunion for him when he came back to this god forsaken valley. Get a clue old man...

Paul
(The Dad)

What the hell was that kid doing upstairs? He was always able to sit still for too damn long. He had not heard a peep out of him since he went up there. He would be useless, just like he thought he would be before he called to tell him that his mom was gone. He would probably sob at the funeral, hide from the relatives and he would not help with the animals. He was afraid of the cows, and he thought the chickens were filthy. Stupid kid. He never could depend on him for anything.

But Laurel, she will be here soon, and that girl can do it all. She can milk and herd and pluck and plow. She always threw on a pair of overalls when she got home, dug out her old barn boots and started working. She was cut of the same cloth as his mom, her grandmother, and that woman was a gem. His mother had kept 8 boys fed and clothed while working 16-hour days on the farm. She never complained and she always whistled while she cooked and cleaned and drove the tractor. Her name was Gerda, and she was a full-blooded Norwegian. Marvelous woman. Laurel was as close as he had come to meeting a woman that was as tough and good as his mother Gerda.

He would get Laurel to help him with the funeral arrangements. He did not even bother to ask Simon. He would start crying, probably, and be useless. Maybe Laurel could let Simon do something like pick the flowers or something. Not that anything was going to be extravagant. He was not made of money and his wife, Doris, had up and died before they had set aside money for funerals and caskets, at least that is what he thought. It would have to be on a budget for sure.

He was going to make some afternoon coffee now. Doris never wanted him to because she thought it interrupted his sleep, but he did not think it did. He never had slept so great anyway, and he thought it relaxed him in the afternoon. Laurel won't mind if he does that. She won't think that is her business. She is just so sensible.

As he measured the coffee into the percolator, he wondered if Laurel would get that new coffee maker out of the shed that she had given them for Christmas a few years ago. He hoped not. The new generation thought everything was throw away, even if it served a good purpose and was not broken. He would tell her he just had to have his coffee percolated. She would see the wisdom in that, he was sure.

Brenda

(The Aunt)

Brenda pulled her gray hair back from her face and whipped it into a bun. She used a hair stick to keep it in place. She had been lucky to have such thick hair all her life. As she looked in the mirror for stray hairs, she saw her sister Doris looking back at her. They had the same sky-blue eyes, the same pug nose, the same wrinkles around their eyes and now around the mouth. She wiped a tear away and walked out of the bathroom to sit down, again, as grief overcame her.

What was she going to do without her sister in her life? How long would the day seem when she could not pick up the phone and give Doris a ring? How sad would the little trips to Yakima seem when she could not swing by and pick up Doris and take her to Costco with her? Who would go to their parent's graves on Memorial Day with her? No one. She and Doris were the last siblings alive and now Doris was gone too.

Brenda could not explain the way she was feeling to anyone. It was like she was adrift, with nothing to hold onto. She just never thought about Doris being gone and because she was 4 years older, she thought she would go first. But why did she think that? Things just do not work that way. Now Doris would not be buried by Mom and Dad, but over in Paul's family cemetery. The smallest thing and it felt too big right now.

Her brother died in Viet Nam, and he was buried by her parents. Robert Nathanial Brewster, Beloved Son and Brother, 1948–1968. Gone too soon. Her parents were ripped to shreds losing their only son and to a senseless war. She and Doris had done their very best to help but they were just kids and the quiet depression that overcame their house made them disappear off into their neighborhood and school days. They were too young to grieve so hard.

Now Brenda is grieving alone. Sure, she has her girls and her husband and some grandkids and a good life. But Doris was so much more than that. She was the one who knew her from the beginning and now to the end. No one knew her like that, and she thought she really did not know anyone else like that. It was sisterhood. It was gone.

She knew she needed to go and check on Paul and to help with arrangements. As much as she did not want to talk to Paul or look at Paul, she had to go. Doris never accepted that Paul was someone Brenda could not stand. She just shook her head and said, "Oh, you know he means well." Brenda did not think he meant well. She just thought he was an ass.

Today was the day Simon and Laurel would arrive and that would make it easier to bear. They were good kids. Both got out of the valley and went to college and had good jobs. They never asked their parents for money or help with anything. She did not know yet that Laurel was staying and had left her job in Seattle. That news would hit her hard.

For her Simon was the favorite. He was a gentle and loving boy who grew into a thoughtful son. He chose a life for himself, away from his family, but not too far. He could still see his mother and sister. He seemed happy, but was not someone who shared much about his life. So, assumptions were made about his life, but she felt her instincts were good.

She put on her old barn coat and walked out

to the car. She noticed the iris' opening along the front fence and she thought of her and Doris, digging them from their parent's yard once they sold their childhood house. They were beautiful, purple and white with a lacy pattern on the petals. She stopped and stared at them for a moment and felt the tears welling up one more time.

Laurel

When the train pulled into the station, she saw her little brother Simon leaning on a railing. His hands were stuffed in his pockets and he was as thin as she had ever seen him but he had always been a skinny guy. His hair was long and pulled back in a loose pony tail and was still the beautiful blue-black color she remembered, thick and shiny. His clothes were loose fitting jeans, hiking boots and a slim fitting sweatshirt in a coral color. She knew it was a name brand sweatshirt. Simon liked plain clothing, good colors, and good brand names. She waved but he was looking away, looking sad and her heart leapt a little when she saw that expression.

She remembered it from childhood. Her baby brother, never quite in the right place at the right time, like he had been born into the wrong family and definitely in the wrong place. She thought of how his first-grade experience had been and how it was the beginning of a rocky school career.

They went to a school that was only a half a mile away from where their driveway connected to the country gravel road. They always walked to school, unless there was a dust storm or a blizzard. Rain really did not happen often enough to even own an umbrella.

When he started first grade, Laurel was in the fourth grade. He begged his mom not to take him the first day and he said he just wanted to walk there like Laurel and keep it low key. Their mom gave them each their quarter for milk money to go with their packed lunch. She hugged them and sent them on their way. Laurel tried to get Simon to talk to her on the way, but he was completely quiet. He looked down and walked beside her and said nothing. When they got to the school yard, she told him she would walk him to the first-grade rooms, but he said no, he knew where they were.

She marched off to her classroom with complete excitement. She loved school, she loved the teacher she had been assigned to and she was ready to get on with it. She did not look back.

If she had looked back, she would have seen Simon exit the school yard, into the parking lot, crouch beside a car and wait for the bell to ring. Once it rang, he bolted across the road, climbed under the fence and disappeared into a stand of cotton wood trees next to a small creek. He spent the day there, doing whatever he could find, which was plenty. He threw rocks, laid in the shade, caught bugs, took his shoes off and waded in the creek because late August was still summer time hot there. At 3:00 when the school bell rang, he snuck back across the road and walked to the end of the school yard, keeping a low profile behind the gardener's shed. When he saw Laurel looking for him, he whistled and gave a quick wave.

Laurel inquired, what are you doing out here and he said, I just wanted to run once I got out of the classroom and this as far as I can run without going home alone.

Laurel accepted this and home they went. Their mom greeted them at the door with warm cookies and a big hug. All the questions about the first day and Laurel answered first on it all. Their mom turned to Simon and said, well, do you like your teacher? Simon enthusiastically said, yes, she is very nice.

So, this went on for about a month. One day Doris was putting away some laundry for Simon and she saw a lumpy sock in the back of his drawer. When she pulled it out it was full of quarters, about 20 to be exact. As was the preferred response in their family, she simply put them in the quarter jar in the kitchen, asked no questions of Simon and preceded to give him a check the next morning to take to the school lunch room to pay for his milk for the next month. She did not ask him why he was not using the money for milk, but just decided this would be a better way to handle it. No need to get the whole family riled up.

As luck would have it the fourth graders and first graders had different recesses and lunches, so Laurel never wondered about whether or not she would see Simon during the day. Then one day her teacher announced that all 4th graders who were in the top reading group would be going to the 1st grade classroom to help the younger students make paper mâché pumpkins. Laurel was assigned to Simon's home room, which she found annoying and exciting all at once. Simon had told his mother that the reason he was not bringing home school papers was because his teacher was posting his as examples of good work on the bulletin board. (He had heard Laurel talk about this ever since she started school because she was top of the class, always!) Laurel was ready to see his magnificent work.

When they entered the classroom Laurel was

looking for her brother first. She thought, front of the room, if he is so smart, but there was no Simon. She looked at the posted work and there was nothing with Simon's name on it. She was going to ask the teacher, when she was assigned two scruffy boys to help with the pumpkins. They were gross. One had not had a bath in so long that the dirt was so in-grained in his skin that it looked brown. His hair was uncut and had masses of tangles in it. He smelled so bad, but she held her breath and introduced herself. The other boy was ob-viously painfully shy and he would not make eye contact with her or speak. She sighed and proceeded with her assignment. Her teacher must have trusted her to work with these re-jects, was all she could imagine.

On the way home Simon met her in the usual spot. She looked at him suspiciously and said, "Where were you today?"

Simon snapped back, "At school!"

"No, you were not. I was in your classroom and you were not there. I looked for you and by the way, your work was not posted on the bulletin board."

"I had a stomach ache and had to lay down in the nurse's office. And my teacher took my work down so someone else could be the best for a while."

Laurel looked at him sideways and decided

she would bring this up with her parents, at dinner. All the way home she kept thinking how strange it was that no one ever said anything to her about her little brother. It was not a big school. Someone would have told her he was a weirdo or something, but nothing.

When they got home their mom presented them with warm cinnamon rolls fresh from the oven. As Simon was gobbling his down Laurel said, "Oh, you are over your stomach ache now?" Simon just shrugged.

His mom looked at him closely, felt his forehead and said hmmm. "Well," she said, "you know tomorrow I am going with you both to school. My check I wrote for milk has not been cashed and I want to straighten that out, then I can talk to the school nurse, okay Simon?"

Simon went white. He left the table and was in his room the rest of the afternoon. His mom did not say anything, even when Laurel started telling her about the pumpkin making and how he was not in the room. Her mom just turned back to her sink of dishes and said, "Just forget about that Laurel."

There never was any talk about it in the family. Laurel did not think her dad knew anything. Their mom took him to school the next day. She got his months' worth of school work and each afternoon he ate his after-school treat with a glass of milk and some homework right under his mom's nose at the kitchen table.

Laurel would recall so many times that silence was the answer in her family for fixing most everything. No need to 'beat a dead horse'. Just do what must be done. It created a culture that stuck with her as an adult. More on that later.

When she stepped off the train there was Simon, with his sweet little boy smile and his arms opened to hug her. All he said was, "Thank God you are here."

Paul

Standing in the dilapidated barn with the sun light coming through the door, with dust particles flying around in the dry air, he felt tired. He puffed on his cigarette and coughed like he always did anymore. The farm, or what was left of it, was mostly a memory. Hard work, disappointments and not much left to show for it.

He sat down on a bale of straw and stared at the empty stalls. He used to keep a small herd of milk cows, beef cows in the pasture, a horse for the kids, pigs in the pen behind the barn, all gone but one milk cow nearing the end of her usefulness and one younger cow just starting to provide milk. He still had chickens as they were cheap and easy to care for. The horses and pigs were long gone and the fields of alfalfa and corn had been sold off.

The apple orchard was old. He saw no reason to go to the expense of pulling out the old trees. They did not make him much money, but he opened them up for "you pick" in the fall and kept a couple of old transparent apple trees in the side yard. They made the best applesauce and some of the old gals from the area always came and picked them.

The garden was going to suffer now without Doris. She kept it up. It took a lot of time to hoe the weeds, set up the irrigation ditches and pick and preserve all of it. He would miss that, unless he could get Laurel to do it. She could if she wanted to.

Everything new had passed him by. The tractor was an old Farmall that smoked and belched each time he started it up. He had the old metal sprinkler pipes that he bought in 1960. He could still water the orchard with them but they were heavy and back breaking to set.

The money they had managed to save was from selling off land and some equipment. If the taxes could get paid and nothing fell down before he died, he figured he could squeeze by. Just barely.

At 62 he was supposed to be enjoying the fruits of his labor, but it was not that way. He still had labor to do and he had to do it without a mate. Sometimes he helped another farmer bring in hay or spray their small orchard because he still had a sprayer. But that was not much. He hoped Laurel stayed and helped him. She said she would.

He heard Simon's car driving slowly up the driveway. He didn't want the gravel and dust to mess up his fancy little car. How you could give a damn about a car that much was beyond him. He shook his head and pulled himself up to greet his daughter.

Laurel

When Simon pulled onto their driveway, she saw the long dirt road ahead and the old apple orchard in bloom and it pulled her back to her childhood. Riding her old bike from the second-hand auction down this rutted road, picking apples in the fall. She remembered how heavy the canvas bag around her neck and shoulders felt and the thrill of dumping the apples into the fruit bin. She could smell the sweetness of the apples and remember the cider her mom pressed in the barn. It was a good feeling.

She was sad to have lost her mom, and so suddenly and unexplained. But she had been unknowingly looking for an excuse to leave the city behind her and return to her roots. Some people say you cannot go home, but she thought she could. It was the life she felt she needed. It was the only one that made sense to her right now.

She saw her dad in the front yard. He was opening the gate to come out to greet them. Simon chuckled and said, "He was not so eager to greet me, Laurel."

Laurel looked at her little brother and shook her head. Sometimes he was so negative, but she knew in her heart, there was no fixing the relationship between the two men. She said, "Just let it go Simon. It is not worth it."

Simon smiled and pulled his car in next to the old Ford pickup his dad had driven since 1968. Even that truck left resentment in his heart, but Laurel practically hugged it when she jumped out of the car. It held memories of driving into town with her dad, learning to shift the gears and bouncing on the rutted roads.

Paul came to Laurel with open arms and said, "So glad you are here girl. Just so glad." For the first time since Simon had arrived, he saw his dad crying. Laurel hugged him hard and said, "Let's go in and have some coffee."

Laurel walked through the screen door and was assaulted with the smell of her mom. It was a smell of clean linens and cooking and a little hint of baby powder. Her mom loved baby powder after each bath, before bed, and to freshen up in the morning. She was suddenly overwhelmed with loss and felt her knees start to buckle. But she shook it off, dropped her bag and headed into the kitchen.

The kitchen was old farm house style. Big with wooden cupboards painted white, counters covered in old linoleum, nicked and scarred. The sink was deep enough for milk buckets and loads of garden vegetables. The walls were painted pale yellow and the kitchen curtains were red and white with apples printed on them. The kitchen table was big and could sit about 8 people. They ate every meal at that table. The table was her grandmother Gerda's. A big slab of maple, with the water rings and scrapes of a life full of children. The chairs were an assortment from yard sales and second-hand stores. The floor was pine that had been sealed with varnish by her mom and dad when they bought the house.

She stepped over to the sink made of old porcelain, but as shiny as her mom could keep it and the dishes were in the drainer, neatly arranged. A clean dish towel hung on the peg on the wall by the window that looked out at the garden.

As Laurel made the coffee, in the old tin percolator, she felt her mom standing beside her, felt her hand on her shoulder and she heard her whisper, "Live for Laurel, please."

Laurel knew her dad and brother did not see or hear anything, but the impact of hearing her mom so clearly made her hand shake and she dropped the percolator into the sink.

"Be careful girl. That's my favorite coffee pot!"

Laurel laughed and said, "Oh, I know that. I didn't dent it up any more than it already is, Dad."

The three of them sat at the table and at first it was very quiet. Laurel broke the silence and asked her dad, "How did Mom die, Dad? Did you know she was sick?"

Paul shook his head and said, "It was quick. Just stopped breathing. I found her on the bedroom floor after I got done milking. Just gone."

Simon asked, "So what did the ambulance drivers say?"

Paul gave him a scowl and said, "I called Bob Newton, down at the mortuary to come and get her. She was dead I said."

Simon opened his mouth to protest, but Laurel put a hand on his arm and said quietly, "Is it important for you to know what she died of? Because we could ask for an autopsy."

Paul pushed his chair back from the table, upsetting his coffee cup, and growled, "Dead is dead. What the hell good would that do?" He went out the back door, slamming it behind him.

Laurel listened to Simon talk about the audacity of that statement, the thoughtlessness of not considering what others wanted, etc. Then she said sternly, "It's money Simon. It's just about money."

Simon shook his head and he walked out of the room and went up to his old sanctuary, the musty bedroom with the old braided rug. Laurel sat at the table and tried to gather her thoughts. She did not know what to do at this moment. She wanted to know why her mom died at 58, suddenly and with no warning signs. She wanted to call the coroner and ask if it was too late for autopsy. It had been 4 days. Can a child request an autopsy or does it have to be the spouse? What if she told her dad that she and Simon would pay for it? What if he said he would not take charity from his own kids? That would be just like him.

Deep in thought she did not hear someone come in the front door or walk into the kitchen. Then she heard, "Oh my sweet girl. I am so happy you are here". It was Aunt Brenda.

Simon

He heard Aunt Brenda's voice and his stomach leapt because essentially it was his mom's voice. He went to the kitchen to greet her immediately. There was no reason to sit up here if he could listen to Aunt Brenda.

When he walked into the kitchen, she was hugging Laurel and they were crying. He stepped in and joined them and the three of them shed much needed tears together. The embrace was the first real chance Simon had to let out his pain without hesitation. He did not know that Aunt Brenda and Laurel felt the same.

They settled into the chairs around the table and at first, they just looked at each other and wiped their eyes and blew their noses with the white paper napkins that were always in the middle of the table, next to the salt and pepper shakers they had used all their lives. The napkin holder was a little metal stand with wire sides and napkins sat upright in it. The salt and pepper were clear glass, recently cleaned and shined. Either their mom did it or Aunt Brenda.

Shakey still, Simon said to Brenda, "Do you know what Mom died from?".

Brenda said that she asked the mortuary and they said probably a heart attack as she appeared to go very quickly. Then Brenda added, "But that is just a guess. She was a bit more tired, but that is just age. I don't know…"

Simon and Laurel started to speak at the same time, but Simon deferred to his older sister. She said, "Dad said he did not think she needed an autopsy. And of course, I think it's money. But really, I think we should know what happened."

Brenda nodded in agreement and said, "They have already embalmed her you know. I did not know she wanted that. Our family just did not believe in embalming, but Paul insisted."

Simon googled embalming and autopsy results and he nearly shouted, "Embalming might not show poisoning, but it seems we might be able to tell if it was a heart attack or some other organ failure."

Laurel shook her head and said, "This would

be an all-out war with Dad. I do not know if he cannot handle it or if he just does not want to know, because for him 'dead is dead'. He is really not showing a lot of signs of grief. I don't know what he is thinking or feeling."

Simon said, "Typical, sis. That's the story of our lives in this family."

Brenda got up from the table and said she felt like baking a pie and then she was going to make some chicken and dumplings. She asked Simon to carry in the baskets she brought from her car. She put on an apron, poured some coffee and started getting everything ready.

As Simon toted in the baskets, he noticed his dad standing in the barn door. He had on an old pair of coveralls and he was staring out into the orchard. He looked lost and Simon thought, "That's him grieving. Silent staring and stoic."

Simon actually enjoyed that afternoon with Aunt Brenda cooking and the house filling up with good smells. He listened to the two women chatter and occasionally stop to cry. He cut up the apples for the pie and cooked them on the stove, just the way his mom had taught him. Sugar, butter, cinnamon, nutmeg and a little cornstarch slurry to thicken them. It was the smell of love and caring and it made him feel grateful for the women in his life. He cut the apples in the exact way his mom did, making sure they were thin, but not too thin. You still wanted a good bite of apple.

Laurel made the pie dough and she still was good at it, even though he doubted she made many pies in her tiny apartment in Seattle. She used Grandma Gerda's old rolling pin that was smooth and worn by years of rolling dough. She wore one of her mom's aprons. It was blue and white striped with a row of red tulips appliqued on the bottom. Suddenly he wanted that apron so much, but he knew there was time for that later.

When the pie was in the oven he stepped out onto the back porch and called his work. Rita answered. He could tell she was chewing gum, as per usual. "Hey Simon, how are you? We heard about your Mama. We are all so sorry to hear that. She was kind of young, right?"

Simon realized he was not ready to talk about anything yet so he thanked her and politely asked to speak to his boss, Nate. When Nate answered Simon started to choke up and tried hard to fight back the tears. But Nate was his closest friend and Nate knew all there was to know about Bellingham Simon. Nate said, "It's okay buddy. I am assuming you need time off. You have tons of time on the books. Just let us know in a few days when you want to return and if there are any projects we need to pick up. Just send an e-mail, bud. You need to deal with your family now."

Simon thanked him and hung up the phone. He loved Nate. Nate had started his own small publishing company and it was thriving. He knew Simon from college and called him and asked him to come and work for him. So far it had been the best job he had ever had. Much better than the book store job and the coffee shop and the landscaping and the endless jobs he pieced together during and after college. He was loyal to Nate's Publishing and Nate knew it.

When he went back into the kitchen Aunt Brenda was stirring the chicken and dumplings and she smiled at him, looking just like mom. She asked him if he could stay home for a while and he said, "Well, I can. But how long depends on how big of an ass hole Paul is..."

Just then Paul came through the kitchen door.

Paul

Paul saw Brenda's car pull in and he knew he had just better stay outside. He and Brenda never did like each other. She was always whispering with Doris and he felt like it was all about him. She never brought her husband Mike over with her anymore and he did not remember the last time he had seen him. She made him feel like he was not doing the right thing for Doris, but he did not understand what it was that he was doing wrong.

He mended one of the gates behind the barn that lead into the back pasture to keep himself out of the house. His two cows were standing in the shade of an old cotton wood, chewing on the fresh new grass that was coming up all over. They were both Holsteins. Beautiful black and white cows. He loved having them. Looking at them he could live in a different world, the one where his wife was alive and his home felt like his own.

Not today. Brenda would be riling up the kids with her questions and speculations and her goddamn concern. Simon would be lapping it up and probably would curl up in her lap like a kitten, if he could. Laurel would be happy to see her, but she would be thinking practically about what they should do next. Thank good-ness for Laurel.

He had stayed out long enough and was ready for a little nap and something to eat. He opened the front door, put his boots on the porch, just like Doris always insisted and stepped into the cool shade of their living room. He could hear voices in the kitchen and of course it was Brenda. Just as he started to go into the kitchen from the hall way, he heard Simon's comment.

Simon looked surprised to see him and then immediately changed his expression to defi-ant. Gone were the days when he could in-timidate that kid. He snarled at him and said, "Well, Simon, I will probably be an ass hole till I die, so you could leave now if you have to."

Simon laughed and said, "I'm here for ev-eryone but *you* old man." He left the kitchen through the back door.

Paul did not even look at Brenda but sat down and said, "I'll have a slice of that pie." Brenda cut a piece of the warm pie for him and set it down in front of him not too gently. She took off her apron and sat down at the table across from him.

"Good God Paul. He just lost his mother."

Paul looked straight ahead and took a huge bite of the warm pie and said, "I lost my wife."

Brenda stood up and stepped into the hall-way, gathering her purse and her baskets. She hollered up the stairs, "Laurel honey, call me when you need me to help with planning the funeral. I gotta get home to help Uncle Mike."

Laurel

Laurel did not hear her aunt. She was sound asleep. She had not really slept since she heard about her mom dying. It had all been action, decisions, immediately making up her mind. And why, she could not have said. It was just her instinct, she thought.

The apartment was not hard to take care of and it was near the end of her lease, so she would only need to pay for next month's rent. About her job, she just did not care enough to give two weeks' notice. She gave one day and took the three weeks of paid leave she had on the books. Her friends were a beer in the evening at a favorite brewery and she left early. Plus, email was good for saying goodbye anyway. She did not have much to pack and she brought what she needed. She even left the bedding. Laurel had been consumed with the urge to run. She just wanted to be gone.

When she walked into her own room in her old home it was the first time she wanted to stop. It was all familiar. Lavendar walls, floral curtains that had been made from a set of sheets. Her old chenille bedspread that her mom let her pick out from Sears. It was lavender and white and completely old fashioned when she got it, but it felt right in the old room, with the rough wood floors. When she was 16 and working nights in the summer at the fruit warehouses, she purchased a rug for her room. It was a big circle and covered most of the wood floor. It was purple and white shag carpeting. The only thing that was missing were her posters and her clothes from high school. Otherwise, the room was a good place to lay down and forget her mom was dead.

She had thought she would sleep on the train, but she could not. She was checking her bank account when she had service on her phone. All good. She was making a list of everything that had to be dealt with at the farm. She was mixing up a batch of cinnamon rolls in her head and hoping she could pick a dress for her mom to be buried in. Her mind was overactive and she stared out the window and did not cry. She saw her reflection in the window and it surprised her. She looked older. She was frowning and squinting and her hair was dirty. It made her think about her hairdresser and how she would not be able to get this bob cut in Yakima. Who would know how to do it? Then she thought, fuck the hair. It makes no difference.

When she saw the apple orchard in bloom, she felt real joy and wanted to run into the middle and climb as high as she could in her favorite tree. It was the best one to climb and she was sure she could still do it. She was strong, a runner, always moving. But she needed to hug her dad and act as normal as she could, although she felt completely abnormal and confused. It would not help Simon and her dad if she was not stable and ready to take charge, so she pushed the feelings down and made pie dough for the pie.

When she woke up it was dark outside. She was still in her jeans and sweatshirt. She had kicked off her shoes at some point and she had pulled the bedspread over her. She was disoriented and there was no light on in the room. Her phone was still in her jean pocket and she pulled it out. Midnight. She had slept for 8 hours.

Now what? She opened her door quietly and looked over at Simon's room across the hall. There was a light on, so she stepped in the hall and tapped on his door. There was no answer. She opened the door and his bedside lamp was on, the bed was not slept in and he was nowhere to be seen.

She crept downstairs and went through the kitchen and out the back door. There were a pair of her mom's garden shoes on the little bench and she slipped into them. The yard was dark, but a near full moon cast some light on it. The apricot tree looked beautiful with the blossoms seeming to glow in the moon light. She walked to the edge of the yard and looked for Simon's car. It was gone. He must be taking a drive or something. He probably could not sleep. She needed to get things done and get him out of here for his own sanity. She knew that.

There was an old lawn set in the side yard and she sat down in one of the metal chairs. It was cold on her butt, but she felt like it would wake her up. She listened to the silence and felt wrapped in cool darkness. There was a very slight breeze and she could smell the blossoms on the night air. The only light was on the porch and it faced in the other direction.

She thought of the times that she slept out in the yard on hot summer nights. Sleeping bags on the lawn, looking at the stars. Sometimes Simon slept out with her, sometimes it was one of her friends. They never were afraid that any-thing would bother them. Coyotes stayed far from houses then, not many raccoons in the valley, no possums, and maybe a field mouse, but not at night. They fell asleep to the smell of grass and old-fashioned roses blooming in the yard. They woke up to sunrise and the start of the heat of the summer day. Their pillows were a little damp, but not much dew, and they scrambled in to have breakfast and get dressed.

These were good memories. She decided that this summer she would put a bed in the yard and sleep out as much as she could. She remembered her mom talking about having a big bed in their yard in the summer and she decided the spare twin bed in the sewing room would be just right. A sheet was all she needed.

As she was lost in memories and plans, she heard a car coming slowly down the driveway. It was Simon in his cute Mini-Cooper, forest green and shiny in the half-moon light. He was driving slowly and she realized he was coasting down the drive. He probably did not want to wake their dad.

She did not know if he saw her but she sat still and waited. When he got out of the car, he shut the door quietly and leaned back against the door. He was smoking a joint, slowly toking on it and inhaling the sweet-smelling smoke. He had his head tipped back and was looking up at the stars. She watched him for a moment. She loved him so much, but she needed to get him out of here before he got too depressed.

Tomorrow had to be the day to start the funeral planning, open house and then send him on his way. He did not belong here anymore. She was not sure she did either, but she was not sure what else she could do right now.

Simon

Simon could not begin to sleep. The room was stifling without a window to open. How had he done this for 18 years? Laurel was passed out on her bed, dead to the world, so he could not sit and visit with her. His dad was in the kitchen heating up the chicken and dumplings. He could smell it and the thought of eating it made him sick to his stomach. He could not eat that farm food anymore.

He slipped out of the front door and left in his car. He did not know where he wanted to go, but he just thought he would drive. He drove for a long time, looking at the new spring crops, window down smelling the fresh clean air. He had some good memories out here on the road. He had one really good friend in high school and they spent hours driving around the countryside in the summer, smoking weed, dreaming of leaving the Yakima Valley behind.

His friend had a convertible Cadillac that his grandpa had given him. It was baby blue with white leather interior, old but still a smooth ride. His friend was Monty Paxton. Monty lived in town and his dad was the post master. Monty was different like Simon. He did not have any siblings and his mom was a school teacher at the grade school. In fact, she taught Simon in the third grade.

He was not a jock or a farmer's kid or a book worm. He was handsome, but not in the way that girls in the 90's went crazy for, not where they lived anyway. He dressed like a grunge devotee and in their small school that was considered "strange."

Monty was easy going and had a dry sense of humor and he really did not give a damn about all the high school clicks. He was interested in getting high, taking a little acid and just biding his time until he could leave. He liked Simon because he was so different than the average kid in their class. Simon wore his hair long; he wore baggy jeans and ripped t-shirts. He avoided all school functions including sporting events. He walked everywhere and that was really considered odd, by everyone. Why doesn't he get a pickup? Why doesn't he ride with his sister in her rig? Why does he dress like that? Is he just stoned all the time?

As soon as Monty got his license, they started their long nights driving all over and talking about everything. They were smart, but not studious. They were interested in anything that did not have to do with farming and small towns.

It was on these journeys at night that Simon began to realize that he was not interested in girls. He was interested in boys. He wasn't attracted to Monty or anything like that, but he felt like he could tell him and be safe. It was becoming much more common for people to come out to their friends, a little less so to their families. So, one night, when the sky was full of stars and the corn fields were eight feet tall Simon decided it was time to get this out in the air, at least with his best friend.

He started out by saying, "Okay, Monty, I'm gonna tell you somethin' and it is probably going to either upset you, make you laugh or maybe you will be pissed. Okay?"

Monty took a toke off the joint they were sharing and said through a haze of smoke, "Go for it man."

Simon started to tell him and he found he was about to cry. Oh shit. Not a good way to do this, so he took a deep breath and in a shaky voice he said, "I am a queer, I guess. But I don't want to jump your bones or anything like that. I just don't want a girlfriend. I want a boyfriend, I think."

Monty started coughing and laughing and howling all at once. "Jesus, you are just puttin' it out there bro! You are just sayin' 'here I am and you can suck my dick' if you are into that.'" He honked the horn and sped up the car and was howling out at the top of his lungs. "Hey world! Simon is gay, man, he is gay!"

Simon would never forget that night. It was the best night of his life so far. They stayed out way too late and drove up into the sage brush to just talk and wonder where all this would take Simon. Monty was a true-blue friend. He kept the secret, but he celebrated the truth with Simon. He talked about where Simon should move to be able to openly date men. He asked questions about what the sex would be like and mostly Simon did not know a lot. He just knew he never had wanted to hug, kiss or touch the boobs of any girl he knew. He just knew that a good-looking man made him feel sexy and all he wanted was to touch a guy all over. Other than that, after all, he was a small-town boy.

Monty made him feel like anything was possible and that he could have a life, just not here. Besides, he did not want to be here, that was already a known fact between them.

Then Monty died. Suddenly with no warning. He was gone forever. He was taking a corner

on a gravel road too fast, slid, flipped and landed on a rail fence, crushing his head. They were
in their senior year. He had dropped Simon off
about 10:00 on a school night and was hurrying
to get home and it just happened. He was gone.

It killed his parents, literally shut them down
for a long time. They both took 6 months off of
their jobs. They had a very small funeral and
turned people away from the door who wanted to grieve with them; everyone but Simon
and a few family members. They never were
the same, ever.

Simon remembered standing on their door
step with his hand raised to knock and not
being able to do it. The door swung open and
Monty's Dad pulled him into the house and
shut the door behind him. The three of them
sat at the kitchen table where Monty and
Simon had eaten together with his parents
many times. They were awkward and unable
to talk much. His mom cried the whole time,
silent huge tears just running down her face.
Sadness cloaked them all. It was not a time
that they could even talk about Monty and tell
good stories. That came later, but really much
later than they expected.

It killed Simon. He was alone again and his
life line was gone. The person he respected
and loved more than anyone but his mom was
dead. He would never laugh with him again. He

wouldn't go and visit him at his college, Humboldt State, dope smoking capital of colleges. Monty would never come to Western Washington University and hike the woods with Simon and eat mushrooms in the dorm. The grief was devastating and he almost dropped out of high school. But he kept at it so he could get out and go to WWU. It was already set up and he was going as soon as it made sense.

Monty was everywhere tonight as he pulled in the driveway of his parent's farm. It had been 15 years, but it still stung like it just happened. He spotted his sister sitting in a lawn chair and he realized, she's my best friend here and he sauntered over to join her.

Paul

He had not been sleeping for so many years now. It was something he kept to himself. It felt ridiculous for a working man to not sleep. He stayed active, he did not think he was a person with anxiety, he just could not fall asleep. He refused to try any pills. He still believed that all drugs, prescribed or otherwise were the downfall of his generation. They took too many pills to try and stay alive for too long and they did not care if their kids were taking anything they could get their hands on.

He hated that his own kids had taken drugs and still smoked marijuana. He never got used to it and he spent hours lecturing and complaining to them and to Doris about the evils

of all drugs. He never went to the doctor, period. He toughed out all colds and would only
drink whiskey and honey if his throat hurt. He
did not do checkups and he had no idea if he
had any kind of illness or not. He did not hurt
too much. Just aching joints from an aging
body that did hard work for his whole life.

When Doris went to the doctor, he told her
it was a waste of time and money. She needed
to just work hard, keep eating good homemade
food and drink a little less wine with her sister.
She stopped telling him when she went. She always just said, "I'm going to town with Brenda." It
was better not to argue with Paul. He did not have
an off switch when he thought he was right.

He heard Simon leave and he heard Laurel
get up at midnight. He imagined himself going
out to the yard and sitting with her for a while,
but it would have been uncomfortable.

The two of them had always talked over work.
Feeding the cows, mowing the orchard, planting the alfalfa and corn. They were cut of the
same cloth in the work and it was a good place
to be together. When she left home he had been
deeply sad for a long time. Doris tried to get him
to talk about it, but he just stayed outside when
he was not working for another farmer.

Simon was hard hit too. He and Paul had
given up on each other by then. In fact, Paul
really did not notice how Simon was doing. He

was just used to the hair in his face, the sloppy clothes, the late nights and he and his mom whispering in the kitchen.

He was not sure why his son had turned out to be so strange. He never contemplated why he could not just accept him as he was. Instead, he just believed that whatever Simon was, he, Simon had chosen it out of spite. He knew he hated the farm and all that went with it, but he never thought of it in terms of how much Simon disliked him. He was a freak of nature and God only knows why he ended up in Paul's family. It was not complicated for Paul.

Went he got up in the morning it was 5:30. He had been awake most of the night, but he was fine. He made the coffee and ate some toast and cheese (like his mother always did) and went out to take care of the few animals he had left. He did think of the kids and he made more coffee than he usually did. He hoped they would not waste it. That was unnecessary. If they want fancy coffee, then they can drive to town.

Brenda

She called Laurel and asked her if today was a good day to come over and start planning the funeral. Laurel said yes, maybe around noon and she would pull together a lunch for them.

Brenda walked out to the barn to talk to Mike. He was working on a tractor and had his favorite music planning; Led Zepplin. He looked up at her when she came in and said, "How are you doing sweetheart?"

Brenda sat down on a bale of straw and sighed. She began by telling Mike she just was not sure how she could begin to talk to Laurel and Simon about their mom's health. She had kept the secret from Paul and the kids, but the reasons to keep that secret were starting to seem trivial. Sure, Paul would not want to hear it and sure, the kids would be angry with the situation. But she knew she had to tell them. She told Mike she was not sure when was a good time. Pre-funeral and risk hard feelings or anger or all of the worse things that can come out when people die. It might ruin the event. But if she waits until after or even later in the year, how angry will they be at her and their mom. It was all too much to process while feeling grief stricken at the loss of her sister.

Grief has no boundaries or sets of rules. Even the books written about the stages of grief do not always resonate with everyone. Maybe you experience anger first or it lays dormant until years later when something opens up that part of you. You might live in denial for a very long time, never really accepting the person you loved is gone. Maybe you think it really was the fault of someone else and that keeps you from accepting it. Maybe you get used to the grief and you cling to it, not realizing the reason is that if you let go of the grief, you fear you are letting go of the person. Grief was a weird thing.

Her parent's grief after her brother died had been terrible to witness. Her mother had collapsed and could not function for several months. She had to be showered and dressed for the funeral and walked to the car. She sat like a zombie throughout the service and when people tried to give her their condo-lences she just stared straight ahead. Later in life she would tell them it was based in the uselessness she felt about the war and the useless loss of her son. She was one who said from the beginning, we do not belong there. We are sending our kids to slaughter. In their small town she was a lone voice, but that did not keep her from speaking up. Their mother had been her own person.

Brenda and Doris had taken over the house-hold chores, even buying the groceries for the family. They washed the clothes and cleaned the house the best that they could. They had lost both sets of grandparents very young and so there was not really family to turn to. One of their mother's best friends, Edna, came around and showed them tricks for cooking and other things. She was one of the few people who would go up and sit with their mother. She brought fresh flowers and German Chocolate Cake that their mother loved. She lost her son two years later to the war.

Their father became very quiet, but he just kept trying to carry on for her and her sister. They saw through his charade but they never acted like they did because they knew it was keeping him upright.

There was a shrine to their brother in the living room. School pictures, Robert in his uniform, baby photos, dried roses from the wreath on the casket, the folded flag in its box, his graduation cap, and a medal he won for some act of bravery. The girls kept it dusted and made sure that they lit the candle their mother put in the silver candle holder she added.

Brenda recognized the grief this time in a way you do not the first time you feel it. It was not as shocking; it was a dull ache and it made her feel brittle and tired. The family she was born into was now gone. She was the only one who could remember the way her parents sat in their matching arm chairs on Christmas morning, holding hands and admiring their children. She remembered the kitchen sink during canning season when it was 100 degrees outside and the big canner was full of hot bubbling water. She could see her mother with the sweat dripping down her face, hair pulled up in a scarf, sleeveless dress and her apron pulled tight around her slim waist. She was hard at work, but she loved the harvest time.

These were things she can share with her children, and she already had done that, but it was not the same as talking to her sister about them. She had been there too and she knew what it felt like to see the sunrise from their summer bed in the lawn and listen to the sound of their mother bustling in the early morning in the kitchen.

She pulled herself together and headed over to the Olsen's house. She grabbed a loaf of fresh bread and a container of cookies as she made her way out to the car.

Paul might participate with planning, she did not know, but it seemed like he would want to help in some way. Maybe he thought writing a check was enough. Even that was not a certainty at this point.

Laurel

Laurel told her dad and Simon to be in the house for lunch at noon. She said funeral planning was taking place this afternoon and Aunt Brenda would be there. She did not give them the option to say no. She said, "You will come in for lunch in the kitchen at noon for funeral planning." Then she walked to the stairs and went up to change.

For some reason she wanted to wear a dress today. She wanted to feel close to her mom, who often wore cotton dresses in the summer. She took one out of the closet that was green and yellow print and had a shirt waist. She had bought it at a thrift store and thought it looked like her mom could have worn it when Laurel was a little girl. It was a little wrinkly from shoving it into the suitcase, but she shook it out and pulled on a pair of white sneakers to go with it. She brushed her thick hair, shiny, cut shoulder length and the same color as her mom's hair, brown with auburn highlights. She put in her peace sign earrings and slipped on the silver spoon ring she had made from one of her grandma's spoons. Okay, now she was ready.

She made a quick call to the funeral home to discuss setting up a meeting to discuss the next steps. To her surprise her mom had already set things in place a few months before. The casket, funeral, opening of the grave, etc., were arranged and paid for. This took Laurel by surprise, but she just filed it under "Mom was always prepared."

Lunch was simple and made from what was in the cupboard. Tuna sandwiches, pickles on the side, and pickled beets from the pantry with cottage cheese. She put on a fresh table cloth with an ivy pattern and laid out her mom's plates and silverware. All set.

She put a notebook on the counter with a fresh pen and a list of items that need to be handled.

Brenda came in first. She had picked a big bouquet of lilacs from their yard and she pulled out a wide mouth canning jar and displayed them on the side board. The side board was very old and it had come from Norway with

Grandma Gerda. It was still sturdy, but there were scratches from years of use. You could still see the Rosemaling although it was a bit faded. The family was large so they had been lucky to inherit it but Gerda had always loved Doris so she left it to her.

Then Simon came drifting in looking very tired. He had not slept and he was really considering sleeping in the living room tonight so he could open a window. He hugged his aunt and sister and poured himself a tall ice tea. Then Paul came in and sat down without saying anything.

As they ate, Brenda and Laurel went over the things they knew were settled. The service would be at Newton's Mortuary. She would be buried in the Olsen family plot. As they talked it seemed things were falling into place as well as the things that had been preplanned. Arrangements had been discussed at some point with Paul and Brenda both because they knew a lot about what Doris would have wanted. Simon spoke up and asked, "Why did Mom make all these decisions at her age? It just seems weird to me."

Brenda jumped in and said, "Oh that is typical of our generation. We plan ahead for this stuff. My parents had written plans that we followed."

Paul said, "Well, we had decided a long time ago about the burial plot. We bought them after Grandma Gerda died. We got a better price than you would get now, that's for sure."

Laurel said, "Simon, will you help me pick out what she wears?"

Paul blurted out, "Now, see here, I have a say in that. I like her in a house dress, maybe even with that blue apron with the tulips."

Laurel, Simon and Brenda all blurted out, "What?"

Laurel patted her dad's hand and said, "Dad, no apron, that is just demeaning or whatever. I mean, she was more than that. But yes, a house dress is good. Do you have a favorite?"

Paul blushed and dropped his head and said, "Blue, she always wore blue."

Brenda spoke up and said, "Her favorite flowers, as you all know, were roses and carnations. Maybe that is what could be on the casket. Rachel's Flowers is close to the mortuary and she has always done flowers for our family."

Paul glared at Brenda and said, "Good God. Roses would be a fortune. We just need some carnations and something green. She was a simple woman for God's sakes."

Simon snapped, "Yes and beautiful and precious and deserving of whatever flowers she loved. I say tons of roses, pink and white, everywhere, all over the place!"

Paul growled, "I am not paying for that. It is stupid. She was a farmer's wife, not a queen."

Simon opened his mouth and Laurel jumped in. "Dad, we will help pay for the flowers. She needs a beautiful send off."

Paul looked at the three of them and shook his head. "What a waste! You are idiots!" He pushed back from the table and stormed out the back door.

The three of them looked at each other and Simon offered, "I will go to Rachel's tomorrow and order the goddamn flowers and I will pay for them and they are going to be fucking gorgeous."

Brenda and Laurel nodded. Simon stood up and pulled a bottle of whiskey from inside the side board, opened it and poured three glasses. "Anyone want ice?"

That made them laugh and Brenda said, "Yes, I will have a double with lots of ice and a splash of coke!"

Laurel said, "I will have the same dear brother."

The three of them drank a lot and everyone was taking a nap by 3:00, on the couch and in the recliners and with the window wide open in the living room. The smell of lilacs and apple blossoms wafted through the room.

Paul

The neighbors were starting to really bring the food. At first it was a slow trickle. Probably because he kept turning people away. But once Brenda and Laurel got there, people started feeling comfortable stopping in and there was food everywhere. He liked food a lot so he ate it. The cakes and pies were especially good. He ate four or five pieces a day.

The funeral got planned and he stayed out of it for the most part. He informed Laurel that he would pay for the casket, internment, and the plot. Other than that, he told her, "I am actually not going to pay for anything else."

Laurel said, "Mom already did that, Dad. You didn't know?"

Paul looked dumbstruck. His only response was, "Nope, didn't know that."

Laurel understood and she knew that between her, Brenda and Brenda's girls (Angela and Carrie) they could put together a nice spread for an open house the afternoon after the funeral.

Paul stayed on the periphery and avoided being with Simon alone. He saw no resolution for their "problem" and he did not plan to try. Simon seemed to feel the same and he just moved around quietly and spent time with his sister.

When they went off to town to pick the flowers, he felt a small stab of regret for being so cheap about them. He called Rachel and asked her to send a bouquet up to the house that matched whatever they picked out and to send one over to Brenda too. He said, just put "Dad" on one card and "Paul" on the other one.

He had never ordered flowers in his life. It was strange and he wondered if Doris had ever wished he had sent her a bouquet. He did not really know if she would have wanted that. She never asked for much with him, except for begging him to forgive Simon for whatever he thought Simon did.

He could not forgive Simon because the problem was not what he had done but what he had become. He first heard about it from one of the neighbors. Their daughter went to

Western Washington University too and she came home and said Simon had joined a Gay Rights group at the college. She said he was a real queer and was marching around campus with signs and just behaving like a liberal idiot.

He came home and asked Doris if she already knew and she sat down at the table and looked at him long and hard. She knew, he could see that. He did not know whether to be mad she had not told him or glad she kept it to herself. He said some things that day that drove a wedge between them and he felt like it never went away. Maybe that is why he cannot bear to be around Simon. It was all too much for him and too much for his marriage.

When he looked into his closet to get out his old suit, he decided that he would wear his clean jeans, a plaid shirt tucked in, his suit coat and his good cowboy boots. He was going to dress the way he wanted and he was not going to worry if anyone said anything. They did not. Simon could care less and Laurel just said, "You look very nice Dad."

He picked a blue dress and brought it down to Laurel. It was a print with forget-me-nots and roses and he loved that dress. Laurel picked out clip on earrings and her mom's white flats. She also got a slip and underpants because she knew her mom would want that. She put it in her mom's little overnight case (pink Samsonite) and took it to Newton's Mortuary on the way to get the flowers.

Paul was ready for all of this to be over so he and Laurel could settle into their new life. He could barely stand the thought of the next few days.

Brenda

Well, she thought, I guess I am not going to tell them yet. Emotions are too raw and it is better to just bury her and let some of the details wait until things had settled. She contemplated if she was being "a chicken" about it, but it was a big burden right now.

She and Doris had not really talked about how to handle it anyway. They had been making other decisions. All Doris did say was the truth will come out and it will not be accepted by everyone. Brenda was left holding the bag, so to speak, and it was a heavy load.

The funeral was going to be nice and it was all planned and handled. She was just going to concentrate on that for now. It was not a time for secrets and drama. It was a day for quiet contemplation, tears and saying goodbye.

She put on her best dress and shoes and combed her white hair and swept it up in a French roll. She put on earrings Doris gave her for her birthday last year and wore her mother's ruby ring. She looked in the mirror and saw her sister and her mother and her grandma all looking at her with a critical eye. You represent us now so look your best. As she walked into the funeral home, she knew she did look the best she could and she held her head up and clutched the hankie she brought. It was covered in roses and it was old, like her.

Laurel

The day of the funeral came and went and it was bitter sweet. The day felt long and everyone was very kind and said lovely things about her mom. The flowers were spectacular and the smell of roses permeated the entire funeral parlor. The minister who delivered the service was adequate, if not just a little boring to listen to.

The graveside was beautiful with sunshine and flowers all around the casket. Her cousin Angela played the harp and her cousin Carrie sang. Everyone cried and she and Simon handed out pink roses to all the people who came.

At home the house was packed and the food was delicious with dishes from everyone. Their dad sat in his chair in the living room and observed and chatted with all the neighbors and friends who came by. He looked as relaxed as he had since she came home and she thought he was enjoying the attention. Hard to fathom, but it did seem like he was genuinely glad to see everyone.

When everyone had gone and the food was put away and the dishes were done and all was back in order, thanks to Aunt Brenda and her girls helping, Simon and Laurel sat in the yard and sipped some wine and talked about their mom.

Simon talked about her gentleness and the fact that no matter what he came home and told her she listened and then did her magic behind the scenes. Just like not going to first grade. He did not know if his dad even knew that happened. She handled it with the teacher in a way that did not embarrass him. She told the teacher and principal that she knew he was not quite ready and felt a month was not too long at his age to stay out of school. It was not because she was the lying type, she just did not want to set Simon up for a reputation all through his grade school years. Because those things happen and teachers talk and parents talk and the PTA and it all just gets out of control. So, she swallowed her pride and told the fib and his academic success in elementary was not affected.

He talked about the time he brought home a puppy from the neighbor's house and did not ask permission to keep it. He just made it a bed in the barn and sat out there playing with it for hours. When his dad came home from a long day of bailing hay and he walked into the barn and saw Simon curled up with a new puppy he did his usual yelling method of parenting. Doris heard him from the yard and she walked into the barn. Simon was clutching a little puppy; Paul was standing over him demanding he return it to the goddamn neighbors and tears were streaming down Simon's face. She stepped in and said "Paul, stop that. I gave him permission to bring that puppy home. It needs a good home and they are having trouble getting rid of all the puppies. He will be an outside dog and no problem. You can see Simon is going to take good care of him!" They named him Jimbo and he lived for 12 years.

Laurel laughed and agreed that mom had been the buffer between Simon and his dad. Because it was a time to talk about mom they did not go into the worst times between Simon and his dad. It did not feel like a good time to relive that pain. They both knew to stay away from it. Simon actually thought to himself, well, when the old man is dead, we can hash that over if we need to.

Laurel made it clear that she thought Simon should leave the next day. She told him she had to sort out what she and her dad were going to be doing and she needed to think about whether she should stay here or move into Yakima or leave everything and go away to Europe, which they both chuckled about. Laurel had never been a wanderer and the thought of her loading up a backpack and taking off for another country made them both smile. When she went to Seattle, she felt like she went to Mars and when she took work there it was mostly to keep from getting used to another city or State or whatever. She was basically a home body.

Simon assured her he could stay because he had time off from work, but he also wanted to get the hell out of there and they both knew it. In fact, by 8:00 the next morning his car was packed and the only thing he put in his car besides his suitcase was mom's blue striped apron with the appliqued tulips on the bottom. He did not ask anyone. He just took it off the hook by the stove and folded it neatly and carried it to the car.

Laurel and her dad stood and watched him drive slowly down the rutted dirt driveway and her dad said, "He loves that car more than home."

Laurel did not respond. She was not going to be able to respond to every rude thing he had to say now or she would wear herself out and that was not what she wanted to do.

What she wanted to do was work physically, think hard, and cook good food in her mom's kitchen. She wanted to enjoy the gardening and harvest this year and not have to think about who else was going to do it. She was going to do it and as they watched Simon's car turn onto the gravel road, she turned to her dad and said, "I'm going to till the garden this afternoon cuz we are late with planting already. Want to help me?"

Paul said he would get the tiller and look at what seeds they had. He strode off to the barn and she went to the back door to pull on her work boots and grab a hat to protect her head from the sun. Mom's garden gloves were there in a basket and she grabbed them as she headed for the back yard. But first, she took her cell phone out of the pocket of her overalls and tossed it on the counter. She thought to herself, I am not going to need that.

Simon

As he rounded the corner of the highway and saw the sign for the border crossing wait times, he let out sigh of relief. Just around the corner and he was home again, really home. His adopted home with its college students, retired people, alternative life styles, the homeless, the families, all of it. He loved the way people stopped for anyone who wanted to cross the street and how sometimes they did not obey traffic laws if they thought it would be nice to let the next car go. After all they had waited so long, is what he thought they were thinking. He loved the neighborhoods and the quiet mornings in his condo. He loved the way the Bellingham Bay changed colors all day and the wind created white caps as far as he could see. He could smell the sea and the cool air blowing down from Canada and he was peaceful.

When he opened the front door, he was greeted by his cat, Mr. Pibbs. There was a note on the counter from the cat sitter and Mr. Pibbs was purring so loud he could feel the vibration in his chest. He picked up the big ball of orange fur and walked to the sliding door. He opened it to let the air in and noticed that someone had swept it and placed a beautiful pot of herbs in a clay pot on a little stool. It was large and had thyme, rosemary, and sage in it. He squatted down and smelled it and was realized he needed some green in his life. Mr. Pibbs rubbed against the pot and looked up as if to say, "I would have put this here if I could have." He had an attitude that he could project as only a cat can.

Simon thought of who had a key and he knew that it must have come from Nate or the cat sitter. It felt good. They were both that kind of people; thoughtful and unobtrusive.

He was emotionally exhausted and as he laid down on his bed, he was finally able to shut off the chatter in his head and he fell asleep until the following morning. When he opened his eye the early morning light from the bedroom window reflected off the water and he could hear the patter of rain. Mr. Pibbs was curled up beside him, snoring, and the blanket across him was the one his mom had given him last year for Christmas. It looked like a bear skin and was some kind of fabric that felt like the softest thing you could imagine.

It was a Sunday and he could relax before starting to call work and checking e-mails. As he brewed his coffee in a real coffee maker with a good brand that he bought at the farmer's market and poured it into one of his favorite mugs he was thinking about Laurel. He could not understand what she was going to do at the farm. He had tried to talk to her about the why of the whole thing but she waved him off and said she needed to think about that herself.

He thought his sister was a very good person. He liked her sense of humor and her intellect. But it was beyond his comprehension why she wanted to return to the farm in the misery of the Yakima Valley to live with a crabby crusty old farmer who needed a wife. He could not shake the image of her in overalls during the day and with her apron on at night and all just to keep his old man from disintegrating.

Simon felt like his dad needed to rot on the land he worshipped and refused to leave, even when it had reduced him and his wife to near poverty. Laurel had access to the bank account now so she could keep an eye on the money. She told him there was some savings, significant, but not enough to sustain him if he lived to be very old. She said it looked like her mom had carefully taken out a small amount each month to cover expenses and what he made from helping out at other farms as a hired hand went into his pocket as cash. She said she did not know where he put it because he usually only carried minimal cash, but she was planning to find out. Her worse fear was it was in a jar somewhere getting moldy or rotting. That had happened with her grandmother's money and it had been a huge process to try and get it restored and authenticated.

Simon was also mulling over his mom's sudden death at 58 years old. What did she really die from? She had come up to see him a year ago, on the train with Aunt Brenda. They stayed with him for 3 days and he thought they were having a great time. They wanted to do everything and he accommodated them. They drove to Mt. Baker, they went out on the Bay on a dinner cruise, they ate at good restaurants and they drove up to Canada to visit White Rock and eat fish and chips.

When he picked them up at the station, they were so happy. They stepped off in their pull-on elastic waist jeans, cotton print blouses, cardigan sweaters, and white Ked sneakers. They truly looked like sisters, same height and size, both with white hair. His Aunt Brenda wore hers long and up in a bun and his mom wore hers short in a bob. He loved them so much.

There was no mention of illness and they both had so much energy he was the one who felt worn out every evening. Had he missed something? Was there any indication that his mom was feeling bad? Maybe her heart just gave out, fatal heart attack out of the blue. That happens. But it was something he knew he would not be able to shake off. It was a burning question.

Simon tried to chase away the thought that he felt like somehow his dad was the reason she died. His mind went sideways with ideas she was poisoned by him or knocked over the head and killed. The only doubts he had was the fact that his dad depended on his mom for everything. Why would he want her dead? What did he gain? No life insurance as they never indulged in that kind of planning. There was nothing to be gained that Simon could imagine.

He wanted to talk to Laurel about it later. He would wait for her to settle in and figure out what in the hell she was doing there, which he was not sure she had any clue of at the moment. She was just there.

When he went to bed, he tried to concentrate on getting back to work, back to his editing and author meetings and whatever else Nate needed from him. But as he fell asleep, he could only see his mom leaning against the kitchen sink washing produce from her garden. He wanted her back.

Brenda

She had started to write it all down. She had a notebook with flowers and a spiral binding that Doris had given her for one of her birthdays. She also included a nice pen and a card that said, "Please write Brenda. You know you want to and you know you can! Love from your sister, Doris."

It was true, Brenda had always wanted to write. She did not have any education outside of high school and she had worked on the farm beside her husband her entire life. She thought writing required much more travel and exposure than she had ever had in her life. What would *she* write about? But, never the less, ideas floated in her brain. When she watched people going about their lives, she often made-up narratives for what really could be happening with them. She would share them with Doris and have her in hysterics or gasping, saying she did not understand how Brenda could make that stuff up. She read all the time and it was very intimidating to think she could possibly write anything anyone would want to read. It just was not possible.

When she started to write things in the notebook, she was thinking about how she would tell Doris' children the complex story of their mother's last year and why things were not shared. Something told her if she had it all straight in her head it would be easier to discuss it with them. As for Paul, he was just on the sidelines. Her sister told her she had been trapped because of her own lack of courage and education. If he did not suspect that then he was the buffoon she imagined him to be.

The account started out as a factual description, but as she wrote she felt a need to separate from the pure fact and to create the characters that were part of it. It was turning into an easy transition. It was too hard to face the facts without some illusion. Had she really vowed to keep such a secret? It was hard for her to reconcile, so the story took on a different narrative and the actors in the story became more remote for her. She found herself scribbling for hours, then rushing to finish cooking dinner or doing the laundry. She was hungry for time and she did not want to be disturbed as she was pouring herself into the "story".

She visited with Laurel at least once a week. She had some real concerns about her niece and the choices she had made and she felt like she had to keep an eye on things at the Olsen home. She always went on Wednesday morning for a few hours. How Wednesday became the day, she was not sure, but it seemed to work for both of them. Paul stayed outside or left to buy chicken feed or whatever he did and they had the kitchen and garden to themselves.

Brenda watched Laurel closely. She noticed she was growing her hair out and she wore it pulled back away from her face now. She was a beautiful girl with big eyes, a small little nose, and a perfectly spontaneous smile. Her teeth were slightly crooked, but just enough to make her look interesting and not like all the girls on television these days. She was strong and lean and she dressed like a farm girl. She suspected she did not dress much differently when she lived in the city. She was always less about the flash and more about the brain. Brenda loved her style.

Laurel was slowly beginning to talk about her life in Seattle with her aunt. Brenda realized how much she had not shared and she wondered if Doris was even aware of the impact it had on Laurel.

It came out in bits and pieces. Brenda asked about boyfriends while she lived there (after all she had been in Seattle quite a long time). Laurel said there were a few. Then she described one guy, Daniel, whom she met her final year of college. He was from Connecticut, upper class family, privileged man–boy and was a 6-month episode in her life. She never met the family he described and she never saw him in anything but designer clothes, although he proclaimed that he was going to drop out of his parent's circle and live the bohemian lifestyle in his adopted west coast home. It sounded as if Laurel had saw through him completely, but for some reason it lasted for 6 months. Maybe it was how different he was than other men she had dated. Maybe it was the fact that he was trying to con himself and she thought anything but authentic self-examination was pitiful. Maybe she was lonely and he was a good lay. She did not really reveal her motivation, but she did chuckle often when she recalled things they had done together.

She told a story of them camping on the Olympic Peninsula on the beach. Camping on Washington's coastline is not for the faint of heart. The wind can be punishingly cold and the rain relentless. When you do get a beautiful day there is no beauty that can compare, but you have to be willing to face all the elements that come with the rain forest. She said she had packed the equipment and picked the location. It was an isolated beach just south of the Makah Indian Reservation and the shoreline was rocky with tide pools. The wild animals were plentiful, including bears, deer and raccoons. An occasional bob cat might be sighted. She loved the fact you could sit at your camp fire and watch deer walking the beach and a bear splashing to try and pull a star fish off the rocks.

Daniel had never camped in a tent and sleeping bag. In his youth he told her he had gone to "camp" which was in Maine and included showers, warm beds and hot meals. She told him she would gather the equipment and tell him what he needed to pack. She told Brenda that she enjoyed the look on his face when she told him what food he should bring, how much rope to bring so they could put it up in the trees where bears could not get it. He questioned how hungry they were going to be and did she really think lentils were that good. He asked if they should take a gun to shoot bears and how many pairs of socks was it going to take to keep his feet dry. It seemed she had delighted in making him suffer the agony of expectation.

This surprised Brenda a little, but mostly she

understood. Privilege was weakness to many farm people and he was tantalizingly weak. He lived in an apartment off campus with everything you could possibly need. He wore Filson boots and carried a Filson messenger bag, pure leather. They cost a fortune. He drove a BMW that had been "handed down" to him from his older sister. He always paid for their dates and insisted because he knew she was "truly" poor.

Brenda wondered if they had used each other and suspected they had done just that. Laurel to see how a privileged east coast brat could handle the ruggedness that underlies the west and he wanted to learn from her so that on his return to Connecticut or when he was socializing with his west coast friends, he could speak intelligently about wilderness and wet feet. Either way it sounds like it was just a short chapter for both of them.

Laurel was a good gardener, as good as Doris had been. Her plants were growing well and just like her mom, she planted a row of flowers between rows of vegetables. She planted zinnias, asters, marigolds and snap dragons. They all thrived in the hot Yakima Valley sun. She grew tomatoes, green beans, potatoes, onions, peppers, cucumbers, pumpkins, squash and an early crop of peas. The garden spot she inherited from Doris was big.

She set up her irrigation system the way Doris had taught her with ditches beside each row (rill irrigation), watered from the irrigation spigot. She ran the irrigation water from the mainline directly into a galvanized tub. The tub had a spigot on the side that ran water directly into the ditches and it flowed out and down the rows to nurture the thirsty plants. All you did was turn off the spigot when your crop was sufficiently wet.

Irrigation was a fact of life in this dry desert landscape. It had been transformed by mountain water captured in canals and piped to farms and residences all through the valley. They kept their grass green and the flower beds and garden lush with the water that came from the Cascade Mountains. It made growing the greatest past time for anyone who wanted to pursue it.

Brenda spent these mornings with Laurel and it helped them both to grieve and to begin to move on from the lives they had shared with Doris. It was a natural fit and during this time Brenda wondered to herself why any of Doris' secrets needed to be revealed. There was some peace in not knowing.

Paul

He milked his cows by hand since there were only two of them. One still had to be milked twice per day, but the old one barely gave him much in the mornings. He knew he should butcher her for hamburger, but he had a hard time looking at her with her big dumb eyes and the way she trotted to meet him when he threw out some leaves of hay. It was just a softness he had not really experienced much in life.

It was like the chickens. He found it harder to wring their necks when they stopped laying and he preferred to just open the pen and let them wander the pasture. If a coyote got them then that was the way of the farm. He knew that when Doris was alive, she had started buying chicken meat at Costco because it "was cheaper and cleaner" than plucking and gutting your own.

He bought some baby chicks this spring and they were now about half grown and living in with the other hens. He no longer kept a rooster. They were good at keeping the flock under control, but he was tired of the crowing and the whole preening around the hens. He remembered when his mother told him to wring the rooster's neck and she would cook him up. The rooster was only about 8 months old, but she said she was tired of roosters and she could get chicks from the feed store. Paul had thought she was getting senile and was making a bad decision. Now he understood her.

He brought the milk into the kitchen and Laurel strained it with a cheese cloth and bottled it up in big jugs. When the cream settled, she skimmed it off. She even made butter about once a week. It was too much milk for them and so she asked him to take it to the neighbors or whatever he wanted. Some of it went in big pans for the few barn kitties that were left and some of it he put in a pan for the chickens. Some of it he threw out, as much as it killed him to do it. People were not so interested in fresh milk these days.

He had sold the milking machine he used to

have and the milk strainer he had for the house. He and Doris had agreed that they could handle all of it without the extra equipment. They kept the big jars and the butter churn.

Paul remembered how Simon hated the smell of the fresh milk and stopped drinking milk when he was only 4 years old. He would throw up if he smelled the milk or saw it or touched it. He was totally disgusted with Simon's behavior. It was the lifesaving liquid for families for years and his prissy son could not handle it.

Laurel was doing a fine job keeping up her end of the chores. The cooking, cleaning, washing, gardening, all her realm. He did the outside work with the few animals and mowed the orchard when it needed it. He repaired small equipment and mowed the grass. He felt weeding in the flower beds was women's work. Laurel did not want him messing with the flower beds anyway. At least Doris had always told him to get his big boots out of her flower beds.

The flower beds were beautiful. Doris had kept so many beautiful flowers. Roses, lilies, flowering quince, mock orange, daisies, wild lupine, bachelor buttons, iris plants of so many varieties. On Memorial Day she had a large bed of peonies that were pink, red and white. She used to invite friends over to help themselves for taking bouquets to the cemetery. This year Laurel called Brenda and asked her to inform the ladies that they were free to come over and cut some fresh ones for family plots. That really made Paul proud.

On the Thursday before Memorial Day there was about ten different people who stopped in to pick a bunch. Laurel stood in the yard with them and provided clippers. Most of them brought their own and they used big coffee cans to put the cut peonies in. They filled the cans half full of irrigation water from the spigot by the house and because the bed was so big, everyone could fill a coffee can completely full.

Then, the next morning, he and Laurel picked bunches for their family graves. They used galvanized buckets half full of water. They brought clippers to cut back overgrown grass. They did the old trick her mom had taught her and brought a broom and a bucket with some soapy water too. That way you could sweep off the dirt on the headstone.

They also cut climbing roses from the yard, yellow and red. Her mom had always laid those on the grass next to the gravestones for added color. It was an honor to cover the graves with flowers. It was a tradition and Laurel planned to help her dad keep it because it was important to him.

As they bumped down the road to the two

cemeteries that they visited, Laurel spoke up. "Okay, Dad, did you pick mom's headstone or did she?"

Paul shifted in his seat and coughed and rolled down his window and acted like he did not hear her. She repeated the question. The reason she asked was because she wondered why her mom would have picked a headstone already. Usually that was done by the remaining spouse. But when she saw it, she could not imagine her dad had picked it.

The headstone was a rich blue gray granite with flecks of shiny white. The engraving was an apple tree with a rail fence around it. There was a rose growing along the rail fence. It had her information carved in it; Doris Lorraine Olsen – August 20, 1954 – May 1, 2012 – Wife, Mother, Sister, and Friend. There was room for Paul's information too. The tree looked like the one closest to their driveway, on the corner of the orchard. The details were beautiful. She wondered what company had made it.

Paul finally said, "Yes, she picked it."

"Just planning ahead again? Good grief, I swear she knew she was going to die soon."

Paul did not answer. He just stared at the road and shifted down as they pulled into the country cemetery where his family was buried, along with Doris.

It was a peaceful place. Big maples and

chestnut trees were planted around the edges and a border of poplars were along the road. The grass was well groomed and the graves were already covered in flowers and plants. This cemetery was mainly full of people from some of the first families to settle in their small community. In fact, it was mostly white people and mostly farmers. The headstones were not as old as you would think, the oldest dating back to the late 1880's.

They spotted the Olsen family plot. It had a stone fence around it, about a foot high. It was large and had three beautiful rose bushes planted in it; red, yellow and white. They were old and had been there for many years. Every fall Doris and Paul had come out to the plot and pruned the roses so they would continue to be beautiful. Currently there were 15 headstones in the plot. You could not purchase plots like this anymore and this cemetery was almost full anyway.

They began the work of pulling weeds, cutting back grass and washing off the headstones. Paul stood for a long time looking at his mother's headstone which was not flat, but upright. It was really the beginning of the plot. His father had died young and they bought his small plot. But when his mother died the boys pooled their money and purchased a double section. They had put up the stone wall and anyone who wanted to secure a spot in the plot could do that. He and Doris did.

Not all of the brothers did. They were a family that split apart quickly as they aged. The only thing that held them together was their mother, Gerda. As she aged and the boys left home and most left the valley, the family core began to fade.

Paul remembered watching his older brothers fighting in the yard, with fists and fury. He remembered hiding under the porch while one of them dragged his wife out of the house by her hair and threw her on the ground. He remembered his mother silently crying in the kitchen while she peeled potatoes. He remembered the bedroom upstairs with four double beds along the wall and two dressers to hold the few clothes they had. He remembered being the youngest and the beatings and teasing he took from the older boys.

With no man of the house, some of the older brothers took it upon themselves to be the disciplinarians. The second oldest, Karl, was ruthless and Paul spent a good part of his childhood hiding from Karl. He always had his brother that was just older than him hiding with him. His name was Peter and he was smaller than Paul and not as tough. Paul took care of this older brother often.

In fact, Peter still lived not far away. He had inherited the homestead from the family when Gerda passed away and still lived in the old house they grew up in. He never married and kept a quiet life. Paul could not remember him ever coming to visit him and Doris except when they picked him up and brought him for a picnic. If you wanted to see Peter, you went to his place. You stood in the driveway and waited for him to come out of the house. Knocking on the door was useless. He would not come out unless you stood in the driveway and let him come on his own.

He was not very smart and his speech was halting at the best of times. Gerda once told Doris that she had laid on the kitchen floor when she gave birth to him without help and the cord was wrapped around his neck. She had been able to untangle it and finally her husband had come in from the field and helped her to clean up. But they never went to the hospital, as they did not with any of the babies.

It seems Peter grew up at home, protected by his mother and Paul and was never diagnosed with anything. The ramshackle house was left to him along with the small amount of savings that Gerda had. The older boys sold off all of the 250 acres and divided the profits and put Peter's in an account that they contributed to as they could. He never could work. Paul would always look out for him. He brought him fresh milk twice a week and when the garden was producing Doris made bundles for Peter.

Doris cooked him things and sent them over with Paul. Doris was the only woman Peter would make eye contact with and Paul had found it very hard to tell him she died. When he did Peter walked away, into the house, shut the door and said nothing.

Well, he knew this is where he and Peter would be buried and he looked over as Laurel placed the flowers on her mom's grave and thought, she will make sure it all happens the way it should.

Laurel

She was feeling physically wonderful. The outdoor work was doing her good. The fresh air and the hours in the garden and yard had her feeling stronger than she did in the city. She was cooking and she was able to cook things her dad would eat but that she also found tasty. She did not enjoy the housework much, but she forced herself into doing it because if she did not her dad would just let it become a pigsty. And who would have to clean that up later but her, so she mopped and dusted and kept the bathrooms tidy.

But her true love was the dirt and the plants. The flower beds were the easiest to keep up because they were well established with beautiful perennials. She weeded some and cut back and picked bouquets. The old-fashioned climbing roses were plentiful and her favorite was the yellow and orange one at the back door. The flowers started as orange and as they opened the yellow centers came through and the orange was a beautiful outline to each rose. They smelled heavenly and all she needed to do was water them occasionally and tie back any branches that fell in front of the doorway.

She remembered when her mom planted that rose and how they had dug it up from her mom's friend Edna's yard. She remembered that her mom went on a pursuit of climbing roses after that and they built trellis' in the barn to hold them all. There was a red and white one that looked like candy stripes and Laurel convinced herself it smelled of peppermint. It was a fast grower and it grew all along a fence that separated the garden from the back yard. It was spectacular this year and Laurel always stopped to smell it each time she entered the garden.

All this was contributing to her good health. All of it was familiar and easy to do. All of it took very little mental effort and helped her to lose herself in tasks. It was easier than trying to figure out why she was here and what had gone wrong in her life. Gardening was not about anything that had gone wrong, so she could push thoughts of her city life away and focus on the weather and the cooking.

She had a few friends, acquaintances, that still lived in their small town. They had come to the funeral and she had been glad to see them, but had made it clear she would not be socializing for a while. She needed to help her dad get squared away, that's what she told them anyway. They were all moms now and worked small jobs or not at all. None of them had left the valley and none of them had gone to college. She was like an exotic creature that they knew, but did not begin to understand. And here she was, back where she started.

She decided one Saturday to see if a couple of them would like to meet for lunch at the local café, Patty's Pancakes. Two of three agreed and she found herself cleaning up and trying to fix her hair to go to town to meet them. Their names were Maria and Carla. Both of them were in her high school class and she had spent many hours with them at dances and in band and study hall. They both were very nice, as she remembered, and they both had married boys from their school. Between them they had 5 children.

When she walked into Patty's Pancakes it was just as she remembered. It smelled sweet like syrup and salty like gravy with a little bit of grease from the deep fryer. The booths were the same and the vinyl fabric was fading on the seams. The tables and booth tops were all refurbished with advertisements under glass tops. The ceiling fans were quietly whirring and the waitresses no longer had on white uniforms and aprons. They were dressed in jeans and shorts and everyone did have on red tops. The aprons stopped at the waist and were black with the logo for Patty's Pancakes printed on them. The logo was a fat little pig holding a tray of pancakes wearing a striped red shirt and a chef hat. She always laughed that Patty was a pig, because the real Patty had been a red-headed lady that was beautiful and slim and looked like Lucille Ball.

She looked for Maria and Carla and found them in a booth across the front. They were both a little chubbier than high school and they both wore their hair long and pulled up with a hair clip. Maria was dark haired and had huge dimples. Carla was fair haired and her eyes were strikingly blue. They shouted at the same time, "Laurel!"

She felt comfortable with them at first. They were just as funny and sweet as they had always been. Maria was married to a truck farmer who had a big operation and sold organic fruits and vegetables. Things were going well for them and she bragged about their two sons who were in elementary school; Levi and Colton. She talked fast and was really catching

Laurel up on her family and her life. Laurel appreciated that there was not a lot of questions for her to answer and she nodded and exclaimed as the conversation progressed.

When she thought Maria was about finished, she turned to Carla and said, "So how are you doing?"

Carla sighed and said, "Not great. I think my marriage is over."

Laurel was shocked and tried not to look it. "I am sorry to hear that, Carla. Do you want to talk about it?"

Carla was crying with no sound now. Her big blue eyes were dropping tears rapidly and when the waitress came by with the bill, Carla turned her head. The waitress knew them, of course, and said, "Have a great day you gals!".

Maria stepped in for them all and said, "We will Bobby! Thanks for the good service."

Laurel was sitting across from them and she wanted to reach across the table to take Carla's hand but that felt awkward. She wanted to hug her and say "Life is shit, I know." But she didn't and she looked to Maria for some guidance. Maria spoke with a matter-of-fact tone and said, "Well, Lyle has always been a rotten husband, Laurel. But you probably did not know that, since all you probably remember was the football star from high school. In fact, he has had multiple affairs, drunk all the time and wrecked his pick up a year ago with a high school girl in the truck with him. I mean he is horrible."

Laurel looked at Carla and she felt terrible for her. She looked like she wanted to shrink into herself and the sound of Maria's voice was so grating all of the sudden. She did not seem to be done talking and she added, "I mean, the reason CarolAnne did not come today was because she was caught with Lyle parked out on our property. It's a mess, really."

Carla made a pathetic little sound and Laurel decided this was bull shit. She spoke up quickly, cutting Maria off mid-sentence. "Well, I don't think this is the place to lay all this out now. Carla, if you need someone to talk to, call me and come out to the farm. We could talk privately. I don't really remember anything about Lyle, but I know you and I know you are sweet and kind and do not deserve to be put in this position."

Maria looked upset and said, "Well, I just thought you would want to know and...".

Laurel shot her a look of disapproval and said, "I am glad we got together today. I think it would be good to do it again. Next time I'm going to make you a delicious lunch and have you come to my dad's place. As long as I am here, we might as well see each other."

This closed up the conversation and when they got up Laurel moved in and hugged Carla. She looked into her blue eyes and she saw how hard things had been on her and she said quietly, "It will get better, but I know it is very dark now." Carla nodded and walked ahead of them out the door.

Maria seemed a bit clueless and said, "Good to see you, Laurel. See you sooner than later!" She bounced out of the restaurant and Laurel noticed her jeans were too tight across her butt and that her hair had a root line of lighter brown hair. She thought, she's a phony and she is just full of her big deal life here in her tiny town.

As she was driving home, she thought about the small-town life she lived growing up, in a bubble with everyone knowing everyone else's business. She thought about women like Carla who married their high school sweetheart and stayed put because they thought it was going to be a good choice. She thought about Maria and her choices and that by sheer luck she was not in a similar bind as Carla, yet Maria felt like she was just the best at making choices so she could just sit and brag her head off while she knew her supposedly good friend was sitting there in agony. And again, she thought to herself, what was I thinking coming back here?

When she pulled down the long driveway, she suddenly felt exhausted. She sat in the car for a bit with her forehead on the steering wheel. She knew she had to start addressing what the hell she was doing here. She just did not know where to start.

Simon

Getting back into the routine of working, riding his bike, meeting up with friends, going to his yoga class all felt good and peaceful. He was immersed in his own thing and most of the day he did not think about Laurel or his dad or his mom. He bought more house plants and vowed to keep them healthy. He cooked good meals and took his lunch to work. He always felt better when he ate his own food. He drank less, smoked more, and appreciated his kitty to the maximum.

One evening he was watching a documentary about an infamous serial killer in Britain. It was engrossing and he was sipping wine and holding Mr. Pibbs. When he got up to pee, the phone rang and he answered and it was Laurel.

"Hey! How are you sister?"

"Oh, okay. I am busy here on the farm, Simon. The garden is bigger than ever. I tilled up more and even put in a corn patch. I have no fucking idea what I will do in the winter in this valley, but for now, I grow vegetables!"

Simon chuckled but heard an undertone of panic in Laurel's voice. He said, "Come the winter you can come here and keep Mr. Pibbs and I company for a while. I could use some company and you could bring some of your harvest... You okay, sis?"

There was a silence before she spoke and she said softly, "I do not know Simon. I just do not know what my plans are for anything. I am just moving in a dusty summer dream I guess."

Simon sighed and said, "Can't you come and see me so we can have real conversations about what you are doing? And Laurel, I am not satisfied with how our mom died. I think there is something that we are not being told. I am even worrying that dad killed her, I mean, really. I try not to go there but it is just all too weird. We need to talk to each other more."

Laurel chuckled for the first time and said, "Simon, he did not kill her. I mean the man is in-capable of that kind of thinking. He is basic. You always make him so complicated. Just face it. He is a simpleton. So, just fuck that idea of him killing her. But I think Aunt Brenda is keeping something from us for sure. The more I think about it, her finger prints are all over mom's pre-planning for death. She has not offered up anything but I am planning to work on her."

The conversation continued and they wrapped it up with promises to keep in touch and Simon did suggest that Laurel needed counseling. He did not get an answer to that, but he thought, I will keep trying.

When he went back to the documentary, he did not hear a thing that was being said. He was wrapped up in what Laurel had said about their dad being a simpleton. Simon was ruminating on this when he started to have a memory of an event from his childhood.

He had been about 12 years old. They were planning to cut the alfalfa in the back 40 acres that was still part of their farm at that time. His dad and his sister drove the swather. It was the first cutting of the year and it was warm and sunny but not as hot as it would be later in the summer. They were still in school but Laurel got the time off to help with the harvest. He wanted the time off too, so his mom and dad decided it would be the year he could start helping more with the harvest.

He was so happy to get time off from school. He was a good student academically, but still awkward socially. He had a few friends that also were that way, but a lot of his day he spent avoiding jocks and big mouths who delighted in making him feel even weirder than he already felt.

The first morning of the alfalfa harvest they got up and ate a big breakfast. Their mom had pancakes, eggs, bacon, ham, and fried apples ready by 6:00 a.m. As they ate, dad talked about what they needed to do after breakfast and mostly he just talked to Laurel. She tried to get him to include Simon and would say things like, "Yeah, Simon, you can help me with that too." And, "Maybe Simon can help mom with milking while we get the tractor ready."

Their dad never took the hint, but as they all walked out to the barn he turned to Simon and said, "This time you are going to drive the tractor out of the shed."

This was shocking to Simon. He had been told so many times that driving the tractor was harder than he thought. He kept telling him he was too skinny, too scared, too much of mama's boy for that kind of work. Simon had never asked to drive the tractor, but Laurel had asked for him because she thought it was time he learned. But his dad's response and had been so mean that she stopped asking to save Simon the embarrassment.

So, now all of the sudden, Simon was going to drive. He was not mentally prepared. All along he saw himself helping his mom milk, feed chickens and baking biscuits in the kitchen. He was not prepared to drive the tractor.

When he climbed awkwardly up onto the tractor seat, he looked at Laurel for support, but she could hardly hide her horror. It was if she could see the outcome and was bracing for it. His dad started barking instructions at him saying, "Jesus Christ, get up there like you belong on a tractor. God damnit, you have to start the thing. What are you doing with your foot? Laurel, get up there and show this sissy how it's done!"

Laurel glared at her dad and her mom stepped forward and said, "Paul, you have not even told him what to do. Stop yelling at him."

Paul ignored them both and continued with his assault. "Simon, I was driving tractor from the time I was 8 years old! Even Peter as slow as he is, could drive a tractor as a kid. What the hell is wrong with you?"

Looking back Simon could still hear the sound of his dad's voice and he could still feel the nausea that gripped him when he realized he did not know anything about starting the tractor and that he just could not do it. He knew it should be different, but he just did not know how it should have been handled. He was used to this abuse, but he was not comfortable with it. He thought he deserved it, but he did not know why he could not do anything his dad wanted him to. He knew he was less than he was supposed to be and the shame was unbearable.

When he threw himself off the tractor he ran as hard as he could down the driveway. He did not know where he was going but he could not stop. He kept running and found himself in Aunt Brenda's yard two miles away and he climbed under her porch and hid. He saw his mom drive up and call for him and he stayed put. Aunt Brenda came out of the house and he heard her say, "I would like to kill that son of a bitch, Doris."

He stayed there all day. He thought of sleeping under there but there were too many spiders and eventually Aunt Brenda's dog gave him away. When she pulled him out and dusted him off, she threw her arms around him and he felt hot tears on top of his head. She led him into the house and made him a sandwich and cut him a big piece of cake. In about an hour his mom came and got him and when he got home, she took him upstairs for a bath and bed time. She did not say much, but the look on her face was of quiet resolve.

In his memory he did not have any recollection of his mom ever hugging his dad again. He remembered that she was quiet and aloof around his dad, but she only talked and laughed with him and his sister. He realized it was the day his dad broke the marriage.

Simon stared at the television and did not register a thing. He was just a boy again and his heart was aching for that skinny kid who could not please his dad. He wanted to never think of these things, but you cannot bury it so far down that it does not come back to you when you least expect it. It was one event in a long line of events that made his life at home miserable. Forgiving Paul Olsen, well, that just was not going to happen.

Simon fell asleep with images of his mom smiling at him as he brought in the iris' and put them a vase, careful to arrange them per-fectly and set it on the side board. He felt her hand on his shoulder and he heard her say, "You are a wonderful person Simon and don't you ever forget it."

Brenda

She woke up a little late and started to jump out of bed like she always did, but she remembered that Mike was away for a few days and she could just settle back into her covers. It wasn't like Mike was the kind of man who wanted his woman up when he was up, but old habits die hard and she had always made him breakfast, just the way her mother had taught her.

The day was warm already and she rolled on her side to look out at the field in back of the house. They had four horses now. They were lazily munching the grass in the pasture. One was under the willow scratching her neck on a low hanging branch. They looked so beautiful with the sun on their shiny coats.

She wished she was a painter so she could capture the morning light and the shadows and the colors of the horses. One pinto, one roan and two palominos.

She had not slept particularly well that night. She woke often and padded into the bathroom to dribble a little pee and then sighed and climbed back in bed, only to stay awake for an hour at least before she went back to sleep. In those waking hours she thought about the predicament she was in with Doris' secrets. There was not just one, but two, and she had kept them locked in tight. What was the consequences for her, she wondered? Was she feeling the pressure physically? Was it just mental strain?

The writing had helped but it did not alleviate any guilt. It was like exercising her mental state into a manageable state, but was it sustainable? Each time she visited Laurel she felt a distance that she did not want. Maybe, she hoped, Laurel does not notice it. Laurel seems absorbed in her own struggle regarding what she should do with her life.

Brenda wondered how that happened to Laurel. She had always envied her niece for the choices she made. Leaving their farming town was a good choice and getting her education was great. The city had always had a romantic appeal to Brenda, but she was in awe that her niece could actually live there and navigate it all. She wondered at her ability to figure it all out and then to get a good job right out of college. She did not see her burdening herself with love affairs and fights with friends like so many of her friend's daughters got caught up in. She was taking care of business and outwardly, they all thought she was happy doing it.

Once Simon had mentioned something to Doris and she shared it with Brenda. He thought Laurel really did not like living in the city. He had gone to visit her and he thought she was nervous and spoke negatively about her friends and her job. He said, "It won't be long and she will make a change. I just do not know what it will be and I don't think she does either."

Doris and Brenda discussed this possibility with each other, but their unspoken opinions were the same. Simon is the unhappy one and he was just projecting that on Laurel. They both knew Simon was more emotional and sensitive than Laurel.

Brenda was thinking how wrong they were as she laid there in the morning light and she wondered what else they were wrong about. The two of them had always felt so secure in each other that it helped to reinforce that their opinions were good ones. After all, they had always been there for each other, but obviously they were not always on the right track.

Brenda was thinking about Simon then and she saw him walking along the road when he was in his early teens. He could walk for miles. People had to have their say about it and most-ly they thought he was strange. Paul certainly thought so. She remembered how he looked with his shiny thick black hair, always worn as long as he could get away with it at home. He was always tall and very thin and he took long strides as he walked. Sometimes he stopped in to see her and they would sit and talk about anything except farms and his father. He did like to talk about ways in which he felt his mom had compromised too much to stay with Paul, but he said there had to be something he did not know in order for her to stay.

Brenda wanted to say to him, yes, there are things you do not know. There are things that you should know and they are important, but I do not think you will ever know them. She would look at his profile with his long nose and his dark deep eyes. She thought he was unusually handsome. Again, she thought if she could paint, she would paint a portrait of him. She imagined him dressed in period clothes, like buck skins and river man shirts or in a western outfit, sitting astride a horse. But he hated horses. He never rode them, ever.

She was lost in thought when her phone

rang and it was Laurel. "Hi Aunt! Do you think you could take me with you to Costco this week? We need some things and I hate going in that grocery store in town. Too expensive, too many people who seem to know me but I have no idea who they are anymore!"

They arranged to go the next day and as Brenda got dressed and walked out to feed the animals, she contemplated telling Laurel some things about her mom. Maybe slowly would be good and not just blurt out everything, but then again, things were already muddled for Laurel and she did not want to add to her stress. It did not occur to her at that time that it might help Laurel to figure things out if she had the truth. It just did not cross her mind.

Paul

Paul was not feeling well. He was having chest pains, strong enough that he had to stop mid-stride and let them pass. He was losing his appetite and he did not want Laurel to notice, so he was forcing himself to eat more than he could handle. Sometimes he would go to the back of the barn and throw up in the evening.

He was tired and he felt dizzy when he got up quickly or bent over working on the tractor. He noticed that he was winded when he brought the cows into milk and lifting a bale of hay was not as easy as it used to be.

He told himself; you are 62. Your dad died when he was in his 30s and your grandpa apparently died at 50. Men just wore out in his family. He had lost a few friends to cancer, heart attacks and one to a nasty farming accident. He had never had more than a cough or a flu and he worked through them most of the time. One flu had put him down for a week and he thought that was the end for him. But he recovered and hit the routines again.

He was hiding out at the back of the barn for a while today because he did not want to answer any questions that Laurel might pose or that noisy Brenda would ask if she saw him sitting still mid-day. He was feeling hot and he had opened his shirt collar up and was fanning his face with his cap. He was starting to think that if he dropped dead on Laurel, she would have to make some pretty big decisions on her own. Of course, there was Simon, but he had already changed the will and Simon was not getting any of the house and what property was left. He had a separate account that he kept that he would leave to that guy. What the hell would he do with a farm anyway? He would just tell Laurel it had to be sold. And Paul did not think it had to be.

He had whittled it down to a manageable place for one person, albeit someone who could work very hard. Laurel is beautiful, he thought. She will find a mate and she can keep this place going. She can enjoy her inheritance and not have to run off to Seattle like she did before.

He did not want her to go away to school when she finished high school. He tried to tell her it was a good idea to work for a while and then decide if she really wanted to be in college. He tried to entice her into just going to the Yakima Valley Community College and taking a job working for the Farm Co-op. But for all he tried, he failed.

Her mom on the other hand had filled her head with so many ideas. He could remember overhearing her tell her, more than once, "You need to take care of yourself first. No man, no kids. Get a good education and when you can fend for yourself, then you can think about the rest of it. I should have done that but I did not know how. You just do not have to settle Laurel."

It made him feel upset to hear this argument. So, Doris had only settled? He did not remember it that way. He remembered this beautiful young girl who rode her horse into town and was a cheerleader and fun and full of life. He remembered how she flirted with him when he stopped by to deliver hay to her dad's farm. She would bound out of the house and follow the truck to the barn. She always helped unload and he would tell her to knock it off, but she just laughed and did it anyway.

He remembered her dating several guys

in high school and when she graduated, she went to work in the fruit warehouses along with all her girlfriends. He did not hear that she wanted to leave or that she was not looking to get married and have a family. Her actions spoke otherwise and he just assumed she would follow suit like other girls in their town.

Paul waited until the fall after she graduated to ask her on a date. He was nervous because he was not the dating type. He had kissed a cousin; he had taken the neighbor girl to the prom because her mother asked him to and he spent his free time taking his brother Peter fishing or hunting or taught him to do other things around the farm. They were the only two still at home with his mother and she was happy to have them with her. They did everything a husband would have done and she enjoyed cooking and working alongside them.

Paul knew he could not do that forever. He wanted more. He wanted some kids of his own and a nice woman to love. But he was a bit odd, having been raised by his mother primarily who was Norwegian through and through. From the food they ate to the way they conducted themselves; they were part and parcel from the "old country" as people said in their time.

He called Doris on the phone for that first date and her sister Brenda answered. When he asked for Doris she said, "May I say who is calling?" Very formal and unnecessary is what he thought, but he never had really liked Brenda. She had been in his class at school and she was always in the middle of every-thing socially. She annoyed him.

When he said, "It's Paul, Paul Olsen." she giggled and must have been standing right beside Doris because the next thing he heard was Doris saying, "Hello!"

They went to a movie in Yakima and went for hamburgers before it started. They ate in the car and it was all a bit awkward. When he picked her up, he was scared to go in, but her dad was a friendly man and he opened the front door before Paul knocked. "Come on in son, come on in. Your date is just about ready."

As things go, the date led to another and another and soon they were comfortable enough to make out in the car on a back road and have dinner with their families on Sunday afternoons. Paul thought it was all going as it should. He always thought that Doris was just waiting for a ring and a proposal. That all went smoothly too. She said yes right away.

So, when he heard her talking to Laurel about not doing it the way she did, he felt stu-pid. Plain stupid and naïve. It made him feel like whoever Doris was, he was not the closest person to her like married people were sup-posed to be. He had failed somehow and he was not sure what he did. That was the story of his life, he thought. I am too stupid to know what I did wrong.

Now this illness was taking a toll on him. He had never gone to a doctor. If he went now, what would they say? He knew there would be tests, questions, judgements, plans and he just did not want to hear anything and especially from a damn doctor. He could not remember what had influenced him *not* to go to doctors but he did know his mother had been a bit of a magician with natural cures. It came from her old life and she never really had enough money for all of them to go to doctors anyway. She had birthed those babies, all 8, at home, without assistance. Maybe that is all it took for him to turn away from modern medicine. It was not something he spent a lot of time pondering, it just was the way it was for him.

He was deep in thought about how long he could pull this off without Laurel recognizing that he was sick. He thought if he could keep up with the chores he had for now, she probably would not notice. But he was wrong, as usual, and Laurel was on to him already.

He would find out soon enough.

Simon

Simon got a birthday present from his sister that summer that changed his life. She set him up for a DNA test so they could see what their heritage was. They knew that they were at least ¼ Norwegian, but what else? Their mom had always said her family were pioneers and they were a mix of French and German, also some British blood thrown in the mix. Simon had always asked who had this black hair and his mom always said, "Oh that came from your French relatives, I am sure."

Simon was not that interested but Laurel seemed really pumped up about the whole thing. So, they both took their tests and then planned to meet up in Seattle for a few days to visit and talk about their heritage. They promised not to look at the on-line results until they were together. Simon just thought it would be uneventful to see the results, but spending time with Laurel was always a treat. He booked them rooms at a nice hotel on Lake Union and arranged to pick Laurel up at the train station.

They went out to dinner in an Italian restaurant in the University District and stopped and bought several bottles of wine for their room. They planned to party and laugh solid for three days. It felt like an excellent plan.

Simon noticed how tanned Laurel was and that her auburn hair had some streaks of blond in it. It was pulled up in a sloppy bun and she looked younger than ever. She was fit and looked so cute in her short summer dress with her Birkenstock sandals. He was so happy to hug her and he swore he smelled his mom when he hugged her.

They settled into their room and opened a bottle of wine. They had a balcony and it was a warm summer night so they sat on it and enjoyed the sparkling water of the lake. Boats were moving across it slowly and the sounds of the city sounded a little distant and dreamy.

Laurel brought out her lap top and said, "Okay, let's see where we come from brother!" He did not bring his out and said he knew that they would be connected as his friends had done it and told him that siblings that have taken the test show up on your DNA results automatically. So, they opened the website and Laurel started reading off the percentages of her DNA.

"Okay, I am 35% Norwegian, 35% French, 25% British (oh more than we thought) and 5% German. And here it says, you match with someone who is most probably a half sibling." She gasped and clicked on the information and up came Simon Olsen.

"Let me see that, Laurel. I know these things are not accurate. What the hell?" Simon read the information and looked at his sister sideways. He jumped up and brought out his lap top and logged in to find his own results.

"Okay, I am 50% Italian, 25% French, 20% British and 5% German." He stared at the results and Laurel jumped up and looked over his shoulder. "What the fuck?"

The two of them looked at each other and then each gulped down the rest of the wine in their glasses. Laurel went and got another bottle, opened it and poured them each another glass. Simon started to speak and his voice caught in his throat. He stared at the Lake and Laurel stared at him. They were speechless.

Laurel googled the company they used and read out loud that they are considered the most trustworthy and stand by their results as 98.9% accurate. She went on to read that as time goes on percentages will change as more data is put in the system. This did not help them absorb the information.

Simon said, "Who in the fuck is Italian that we know? I mean, I did not know anyone Italian growing up. I mean we did not even have a milk man or what do they always say, 'he's the mail man's kid'."

Laurel was chewing on her lip and looking very serious. She stood up and paced around the hotel room, talking out loud. "This is crazy. There is nothing that ever happened in our boring lives that would have meant our mom screwed some Italian guy. When would she have got away from the damn farm? I mean, does dad know? Brenda? I mean who do we ask now. Fuck, fuck, fuck!"

Simon said, "It cannot be true. But think, I always have looked different, acted different, I mean, dad has always hated me. He knows. I bet he knows and that is why I always got treated so second class. Yeah, he just agreed to raise the bastard kid so he would not have to face the community of vicious gossips..."

Laurel shrieked, "We do not know anything! This is terrible." She picked up his lap top and then she turned to him with a horrified look on her face. "Simon, you have another half-sister besides me."

The two of them sat down on the end of one of the beds and Simon started crying and Laurel did too. All pretense of being strong or tough or whatever a person has to be in their life, was gone. It was a bare bone feeling of betrayal, shock, and denial all wrapped into one horrible realization. Their mom lied, was their dad part of it, do they know the Italian, were they still solid siblings, who else knows, does the other half-sister know about them...

After the crying, they settled in for hours of talking. Laurel put on her pajamas and Simon slipped into his shorts. They sat up, propped on pillows and started trying to remember anything that could have helped them understand this news. They grasped for signs and speculated about their mom's time with an Italian and how did it happen in their little town. The night flew by and when the sun was rising and turning the Lake into a shimmering deep blue, they both fell asleep full of wine and unanswered questions.

Simon woke up first about 10:00 and he quietly showered and made them some coffee. He drank his on the balcony. He felt untethered, like he could float off the balcony and just pop like a balloon into thin air. Who was he anyway?

When Laurel woke up at 11:00 she suggested they go for a long walk and find some food. As they walked toward the city, Laurel looped her arm through Simons and laid her head on his shoulder. She finally said, "Look, baby brother, you are all mine and this shitty information doesn't change that. We will get to the bottom of it. I say, start with Brenda."

Simon nodded his head and took a deep breath. He was starting to feel strangely relieved and he just knew his dad was privy to it all. It would explain so much about the way he treated him.

They spent the next two days together and if anything, the bond they had was growing stronger. Laurel even thought, selfishly, that other woman who was his half-sister could not replace her. No way.

Brenda

She felt obligated to check in on Paul since Laurel went to Seattle to see Simon. She did not relish the thought, but at least popping in for a few and maybe bringing over some food would be enough. She put together a casserole and hollered at Mike, "Be back soon, I hope!"

It was a short drive and it was a hot morning. The sun was baking down on the dry roads and the dust fish tailed behind her car. She admired the neighbor's corn field and the poplar grove they had planted down the length of their driveway. She felt good today and she had some things to accomplish at home, so she was ready to drop the food and get on with the day.

When she pulled in the dusty driveway she

could not help but remember all the visits with dear Doris. Her sister would often be in the yard tending the flowers or bent over the garden inspecting her crops. She imagined her shimmering in the summer morning sun, waving hello and walking toward the car.

Instead, there was no one to greet her. She parked beside Paul's pick up and threw open the gate to the yard. It had a nice familiar sound to it and she latched it behind her, click. Why, there was no reason, but she always shut gates and cupboard doors, crisply moving through tasks as always.

She went in the backdoor, saying, "Good morning, Paul. Are you in here?" She noticed there was no coffee on the stove and that there were no dishes in the sink. Strange as he had been here a few days alone. He never did the dishes, but he always ate.

She sat the casserole on the counter and walked down the hall and stepped into the living room. The light was dappled on the floor and the braided rug that covered most of it. The trumpet vine growing across the top of the window outside on one of Doris' handmade trellises was in full bloom and the orange blossoms gave the room a beautiful glow. She was thinking how Doris was so good with planting and had always made everything work to support an aesthetic in her yard and home. Then she saw Paul.

Paul was sitting in his overstuffed chair. One foot was on the ottoman in front of it and the other had slid off of it. She could smell him. He must not have been washing and he looked like he had been sitting there for days. He was alive, but he could not speak to her. "Paul, what is going on here?"

He tried to form a word and he tried to use his arms to help him but his left side was not moving and his movements were jerky on the right. He had drool on his chin and his left eye was half way shut. Brenda stood dumbfounded for a brief second. Then she said, "Oh dear. Oh dear. You have had a stroke, oh Paul, oh no. What the hell? I should have come over earlier. Oh my God!"

She first tried to move him so that he could get comfortable but he was dead weight and she could not help him. She also noticed he had soiled his pants and he was looking at her with a pathetic helpless look she had never seen from this tough farmer.

She pulled out her phone and dialed 911. The ambulance took 20 minutes.

She paced the living room floor and looked from Paul, to her watch, to her phone and back. She was in a state of disbelief, but at the same time fully aware that this meant she had to remain calm and contact the children. But she waited to call them. She felt getting to the hospital was more important. She called Mike and told him what was going on and he said he would meet her at the hospital, just ride in the ambulance with Paul.

As she waited, she flashed to Peter, the poor brother who could not function without Paul. She did not know what to do about him. He was cut off from everyone now but Paul. Oh my God. What a mess. And Doris barely gone. What a terrible year.

Paul continued to stare straight ahead, but he had that look on his face of fright and disorientation. She talked to him softly and tried to think of what to say. "Paul, the ambulance is on its way. Everything is going to be all right. You just do not have to worry. Mike and I will help you. I will call the kids as soon as we get to the hospital. You are going to be all right Paul."

She felt a sinking in her heart and thought, nothing is going to be all right and you will be dead and gone before it ever gets right again.

When they got to the hospital he was whisked away into the emergency room and she and Mike were left to wait. She explained her connection to him and asked to be there with him, but they said she could not be in the room as there was too much going on and they needed the space.

Mike held her hand and they thought back

to how many times they had sat in this same emergency room for other family emergencies. It all comes flooding back and the smell and the sounds were instantly recognizable. It is like coming home to a nightmare.

When a doctor stepped out to talk to them, they said, "We need someone here who can make decisions. He does not have any type of paperwork filed here at the hospital that would indicate his wishes. At this time, it is a matter of life support or letting him go. Who is the closest relative?"

Mike took over and explained where the children were and Brenda dialed Laurel's number. Laurel answered quickly. Brenda recognized the background noise as a restaurant and said, "Honey, bad news over here. Your dad has had a major stroke. We are at the hospital in Yakima. You need to be here as fast as you can get here. Mike and I will stay put. Can Simon drive you back?"

She heard some conversation with Simon and then Laurel said, "We will be there in less than 3 hours. Hold on Auntie."

Strangely, Brenda thought at that moment, I am not going to tell them anything about their mom now. They will have so much to take care of, they just need to focus on the present. I am not dragging up the past. She felt a terrible feeling of relief and guilt and sat down hard and put her head in her hands. The thought ran through her head that she just did not have enough energy to do all that she was going to have to do now. She just could not face anymore trauma for now and she let herself cry softly, which was not in her play book for being strong in the face of tragic events. She could not hold it together for now. Better to cry when the kids are driving home, she thought. They don't need a blubbering aunt.

Laurel

The drive to Yakima felt like it took a few minutes. It really took 2 ½ hours but it just flew by. It had been such an emotional couple of days and now just as they were developing a plan about how to handle the news about Simon's paternity, they get this news out of left field.

Simon was driving and he was relatively quiet. Laurel was not sure what was going through his head, but she knew it was going to be hard for him to deal with whatever happened to their dad. Too many unresolved issues and unanswered questions and all just on the heels of their mom's death.

She looked out the window at the familiar

interstate. She had driven it many times and rode buses and trains to go see her folks for the past years. She knew what rest stops were the best and she could time her need to stop by limiting the water and how many snacks she would need to get there. None of that happened this morning.

They threw their clothes into their suitcases and hastily told the front desk to send them their bill via e-mail. They stopped and fueled up in Issaquah and while she pumped the gas, Simon quickly called Nate and asked him to go and feed Mr. Pibbs and please let the cat sitter know he needed her for a bit longer. How long, he was unsure.

Laurel was trying to picture her dad with a stroke and she tried to call Brenda again for some details. But they were out of range of a cell tower and she knew hospitals frowned on cell phones. She asked Simon what he thought happened and he said, "I don't have any idea, but just remember. He *never ever* went to a doctor. Maybe this was just years of neglect all balled up in one stroke."

Laurel nodded her head and said, "He has not shown any signs of slowing down, but I did see him sitting in a lawn chair behind the barn the other day, which he never does. I just thought he's tired and doesn't want me to know. You know, all Norwegian stoic..."

Simon sighed and said, "Men die young in his family, Laurel. Maybe he's not gonna come out of it." What he was thinking was, now I cannot ask him about my real dad, if he knew, does he care, is it what went wrong between them, did he kill mom? He knew that was self-ish, but he felt selfish and alone right now. He loved his sister to pieces, but it was not her heritage that was turned upside down. She was the real child. He was only half real. He was slipping into a deeper depression than the one he usually half existed in. He saw it coming toward him like a black cloud. Black Italian hair and black thoughts all crashing to-gether in his mind.

Laurel was thinking about the farm. She was trying to wrap her mind around the fact that if he was dying, she was really going to have to put off this stupid indecisive crap she had pulled herself into since her mom died. She was having an aerial view of the place in her mind, seeing the orchard that needed mowing, the garden growing full tilt, the two cows standing in their pasture, the barn and the shed. She saw the grass around the house green, with sprinklers at the end of the hoses, watering it with the irrigation water and keep-ing it an oasis in the dry landscape. She saw the chickens pecking in their chicken run and the hawks eyeing them from the tops of the chestnut trees. What was it without her mom and dad? Was it really home? Could she do it? Did she want to?

The two of them, lost in their own thoughts, stepped out of the car in the hospital parking lot. Laurel ran in and Simon stretched and walked in. They were greeted by Mike and Brenda. Mike hugged them both and Brenda took their hands and said, "He is on life support. They will need to have you make the decision about letting him go."

Simon heard himself say, "Well, I am not his son, so Laurel needs to do that."

Laurel was surprised, but she knew his pain was new to him and it was so close to the surface he could not tamp it down. Brenda and Mike were shocked and Brenda started to say something and Mike touched her shoulder and said, "They need to see you both. Room 345, third floor. Go on and we will be right behind you."

Laurel took Simon's hand and squeezed it and they all four walked to the elevator. Brenda led them down the hallway to the room. She and Mike stood outside while the two of them went in.

Laurel was not sure what she expected to see, but the sight of her dad buckled her knees. She grabbed Simon to steady her. Paul was gray in color. His eyes were closed and the left side of his face was drooping. He had tubes hooked

to him and his breathing was slow with oxy-
gen assisting him. The monitor beside the bed
showed numbers and lines and neither Paul or
Laurel was certain of what they were looking
at. A nurse followed them in and then a young
doctor. He looked so familiar to Laurel, but she
did not have time to wonder if she knew him.
He stood on the opposite side of the bed and
started to describe their dad's situation.

He had a massive stroke, probably 24–36
hours ago. Too much time had passed for them
to intervene in any way that would improve
his chances of recovery. They were keeping
him stabilized so that the family could come
and make some decisions about the next step.
Simon spoke first, "So pull the plug or let him
be a vegetable?"

The doctor spoke very slowly and deliber-
ately, as was the method to use when a family is facing horrible choices. "That is basically
true, but if we do not unhook his life supports,
he will still pass within less than a week. We
just need you to decide what you think is best."

Laurel sat down on a chair and stared at her
dad and said, "We have to let him go. He would
want that. He believes in life after death and
his wife and mother are waiting for him. He
has told me that many times..."

She felt herself rising up to the ceiling and
looking down on herself. There she was, this

slim little woman with her hair untidily pulled up on her head and her hands grasped together in her lap. She looked insignificant considering the situation she found herself in and she felt angry that she had chosen to be this person, always alone, always strong. Then just as quickly she was back in herself and sobbing softly. Paul was dead in a couple of hours.

Simon

Simon had no words for what he was feeling. Of course, there was grief and loss, even though his relationship was always problematic with Paul. But he was also angry and frustrated. He resented the need to do everything that was in front of them right now. He wanted to go home to Bellingham immediately and start trying to process his paternity, not the death of this man who had been a crappy father regardless of whether he knew about Simon's biological dad or not. He did not want to hear words of sympathy from anyone and he did not want to hug his Aunt Brenda, who kept trying to hug him. He stiffened up and turned away much to her shock.

He loved Laurel and wanted to help her, but she had moved this death to the forefront, like he could just ignore the issue of who is real dad was so they could take care of burying this old farmer. He found himself resenting her efficiency and her clear-headed approach to it all. He just wanted to get the fuck out of there.

They pulled in the driveway that evening after he was pronounced dead and they called Newton's Mortuary to pick him up at the hospital. They had not eaten anything and so Uncle Mike picked up some fried chicken and sides to bring back to the house. Simon thought, I hate fried chicken, but what else do you eat in this stupid family? Fried chicken is comfort food, grief food, greasy and tasty... Paul would be right there gobbling it up if he was not dead in a bag in a mortuary cooler.

When they walked in the back door it smelled horrible. They smelled urine, defecation, and stale coffee. The casserole Brenda had brought had to be thrown out from sitting in a hot kitchen with a lid on it and it had chicken in it, so good bye casserole.

Mike walked in the living room and said, "We have to get this chair out of here now. Simon, you grab the back, I'll take the front." It went down the hall, out the front door and around to the back of the house.

Simon looked at Mike and said, "Let's burn it."

Mike looked at him sideways and said, "Hey buddy. I know you are upset but let's just hold off on that. It might just be too much for your sister."

Simon shook his head and said, "Yes, we must not upset the only kid he ever had."

Mike reached over and put his hand on Simon's shoulder. "There is time for that story. Let's just get through all of this first."

Simon knew the logic in that, but he was so filled with anger he did not want to seem agreeable. But after all, it was Uncle Mike, the nicest guy he knew growing up and he was a man who had handled his life well, so, yes, just listen to him, he thought.

Mike said, "I have to check on the cows and chickens. You go ahead and have something to eat."

When he went through the back door, there were some plates on the table and the food was lined up down the center. Brenda was making some lemonade and Laurel was just sitting there staring. Mike went back in the living room once he came in and they heard vacuuming, scrubbing and assumed he was just getting it back in shape.

Simon sat down and tried to pull himself together and not snarl at Brenda and Laurel. Suddenly they represented everything he hated about this situation. They just acted like it was just another tragedy to bear and of course they would bear it and they would be good at it. Strong, making decisions and letting their feelings take a back seat.

Simon wanted to say things out loud. He wanted to say, "I hated that old man you know and I am so glad he is not my real father. He never was nice or kind to me and he never treated my mom like she deserved. I don't care if we burn him on a wood pile or stick him in a hole. I just know he was somehow responsible for mom dying so young and I think he just got his due now. Ha-ha. No living here with his dear daughter taking care of him just like he still had a wife. He made me sick."

All of this was burning inside his gut and when he was offered chicken, he shook his head no and drank some overly sweet lemonade. He got up and walked out to the garden and pulled himself some carrots and picked some tomatoes and stood there eating them in the evening light.

The garden brought his mom back to him and he thought he saw her briefly, standing at the end of a row of flowers and she was looking straight at him. She was shimmering in a blue dress and he could look through her, but she was really there and he knew it. He wanted her to speak but she faded quickly. He believed in spirits and he felt like she was there to try to help him. She knew he was in agony and the look on her ghostly face was one of despair.

He found himself saying out loud, "I will make it through mom. I will."

When he went back into the house everyone was still in the kitchen, like they could not figure out what to do next. He said, "I am tired. I'm going to sleep in the yard. Laurel turned to him and said, "I will too." He looked at her with a sadness and shook his head. "I just need a little space, Laurel."

He found the extra mattress in the sewing room and drug it outside. He grabbed a pillow and blanket off his bed and went to the side yard where the early morning sun would not be quite as intense. He laid on his back and looked up at the sky and the stars and thought, "I am young. I am going to get through this and be okay." But he knew it was not enough to say that. It was not going to be okay any time soon.

He heard Brenda and Mike drive away and he saw the light go on in Laurel's room. He was not sure he would sleep at all, but the cool night air and the star lit sky were good company for now. When he woke up it was still dark, but a faint lightness was in the sky. It was a beautiful time of morning and he got up and started walking, just like when he was a kid.

Laurel

When Mike and Brenda left, she walked into her parent's room and looked out the window at her brother, laying on the twin bed mattress in the side yard. Her heart ached for him, but she knew he had to do this process his own way.

For her, she had to take care of some business before she did anything like decision making about the future. There were so many questions and she wished she had asked her dad some things, but then she did not think he would die only a few months after her mom.

She sat down on her parent's bed and looked around the room. It was just as it had always been her whole life. The curtains were white Cape Cod style with tie backs. Her mom loved pale blue, so the walls were painted blue and the bed spread was a quilt her mom made in shades of blue and yellow. It was appliqued with each block depicting a different flower in shades of blue. The sashing was yellow and the back of the quilt was a sheet with yellow roses printed on it. She felt for the little tag her mother had embroidered and sewed on the back. It said "August 2000, Quilted by Doris and Brenda". Her mom loved this quilt and worked on it for two years before she and Brenda quilted it. Laurel thought, I guess it is mine now. That thought brought buckets of tears and she laid back on the bed and let herself be enveloped in grief.

When she sat up, she felt the soft carpet under her bare feet. That had been done several years ago and had been a present from her to her mom. Doris had mentioned in passing that the floors were so cold in the bedroom when she got up to use the bathroom at night and she always had wanted some carpeting in there.

Laurel had called a carpet store in Yakima, asked them to go and measure and then took the train over and rode with her mom and Brenda into Yakima to pick the carpet. Of course, Paul was having a fit and making it miserable, but the women moved forward in spite of him. Doris picked a plush pale blue carpet and Laurel insisted they get the thickest padding. Her mom did not know much about carpet. Laurel did not either, but she had consulted some of her friends who insisted on having everything "just so" and that tip came from them. They had told her do not scrimp on anything because the way you describe your mom it might be her only carpet.

As she looked down at the carpet in the twilight from the window, she saw that it was still in good shape and there were no stains. She was so glad she had done that when she did. She had no idea then that her mom would have a relatively short time to enjoy it.

She stopped in the living room and looked at the blank space where the chair had sat. She could see her dad sitting there, relaxing after a long day. She remembered climbing up on his lap when she was little and resting her head on his shoulder. She thought of him sitting there at his wife's funeral, man of the house, happy for a good turn out to remember his Doris. She saw him asleep before the sun set these last few months with his head thrown back and snoring. She felt his hand on her shoulder and she knew he was in the room with her, remembering and assuring her he was all right.

When she switched off the lamp in the hall way and headed up the stairs, she tried to let in a thought about what she was going to do about this place, but she was too tired to let it in. Her life had just taken another drastic turn in a very short period of time and she wondered how clearly, she would be able to think this through. Coupled with the discovery that Simon was not her dad's son, she felt like she was drowning in uncertainty.

She saw her bag from the Seattle trip tossed on the bed. She remembered packing and feeling so happy to be meeting up with Simon and just enjoying her old city like a tourist. She had packed light for three days and had been feeling ready for fun when she was leaving.

If a person knew what was in store for them at any given time it would be impossible to prepare. Peaceful and contemplative sound very wonderful, but how much of life is really like that? Laurel laid down on her bed, fully clothed and fell into a deep sleep.

Brenda

Her mind was a jumble. She wanted to think practically and help with all that was ahead in the next few weeks, but she was lost in the past. She was rewinding conversations she had with Doris through the years. So many of them.

She was thinking about how Doris felt about not being a grandmother. She was devastated. When she preached to Laurel the good sense of getting an education, taking care of yourself financially, she thought she had forgot to add, then meet a nice man and make a family. She told Brenda she was sure she had never said that to her, but must have felt it was implied. She lamented, "I made my regrets her dreams and I regret it now; more regrets!"

Doris had tried to comfort her but she had two daughters that stayed in the valley and married young and she had five grandchildren. They all lived within a two-mile radius from her and Mike. Each time one was born she resented how exciting it was to her sister, but Doris was sweet and she knitted blankets and sewed baby quilts for all of them. If she was envious or sad about it, she never let on. She was unselfish like that.

Brenda never told Laurel or Simon how much their mom wanted grandchildren. She promised Doris, she would never mention it. Doris knew Brenda was prone to blurting out uncomfortable truths in family settings that made everyone feel bad or just uncomfortable. So, she made it very clear that this was not a topic to ever bring up to the siblings. Brenda had refrained although there had been several opportunities.

Now both Paul and Doris are gone and there won't be grandparents even if either of them ever decided to have children. Laurel was 36 now and although people were having children later and later, Laurel did not even have a partner of any sex. She seemed to be enjoying some weird celibacy. Of course, Simon could become a parent, but he too had no partner or seemed to ever of had one. Brenda found it so strange.

She reminded herself of how successful

both of them had been in careers. They made enough money to never have to ask for help, but with her girls, well, she and Mike kicked in help often. She had bought car seats, cribs, preschool tuitions, swing sets, etc. She would fantasize about having all that money in a savings account now and how she and Mike could go on exciting vacations and maybe own a condo somewhere on the ocean. But the Sunday dinners, birthday parties, and picnics were all such wonderful memories and there was so much more to come. After all, it was just money, not experiences. Her experiences as a grandmother were wonderful.

She thought about how her sister put all of her efforts into getting her children out of the valley and away from the life she had lived. She remembered when Doris drove Laurel to 5 different colleges to look at campuses and poured over curriculum options with her. They stayed on the west coast, Oregon, California and Washington, but Doris was the one who could keep up the visits and paid for them with what little money she and Paul had between them.

Simon had just decided for himself long before it was time to visit schools. He worked hard to get scholarships and applied to Western Washington University and never looked back. Like so many people who went to Bellingham for college, he never left. It was everything he loved and it was right where he wanted to be. Close to Canada, close to big cities, close to mountains, on the water, close to hiking and camping. Perfect. And of course, a place where his homosexuality was not an issue.

Doris had been the architect that drew up the plans for their lives, but most especially Laurel's. It was so obvious from the time he was little that Simon would never be a farmer. He was cut of a different cloth, as they say. Doris had never told him just what cloth, but he was getting closer to the truth now.

When Brenda had heard that Laurel bought the DNA test kits for her and her brother, she had wanted to warn them. As she thought more about it, she told herself that maybe Simon would be relieved and happy to find out he was not an Olsen. Of course, there was the chance he would be angry realizing how deceitful his mom had been for so many years. From his reactions when he came to the hospital and later at their house, it was obvious the later was where he was at. The death of Paul was not beneficial to working out these feelings and she felt sick inside that she had not just told them everything before this, but hind sight and all, all that was left was regret. More damn regret.

Mike brought up Peter, Paul's brother, on the way home and said, "We have to go there tomorrow and talk to him. I don't even know if he takes care of his own money or anything. I just know he cannot stay in that old run-down house forever."

Brenda sighed and said, "Can you do that? He is so uncomfortable with women. I will help Laurel find about the care taking. It must be in Paul's finances or in his will or something."

When they went to bed that night, Brenda stared at the ceiling for what seemed like hours and tried to get back to practical matters, but she was lost in the past. She saw Doris at 25, pregnant with Simon, standing in the kitchen, elbows in the soap suds and tears running down her face. Little Laurel was playing with the kitty in the sunshine coming through the screen door. Brenda was taking a loaf of bread out of the oven and telling Doris everything was going to be all right, she would see, and no one will ever know about Diego.

Simon

When he walked back down the driveway past the apple orchard, he knew what he was going to do. He walked into the shed by the barn and grabbed a gas can. He had a lighter in his pocket. He walked to the back and took one look at the chair and poured gasoline all over it, giving it a good soak. Then he grabbed one of the hoses and turned on the water, just in case the fire got out of control. He did not move it off the green lawn. It would grow back quickly in this heat and with good irrigation water from a sprinkler.

He lit a rag from the shed and tossed it onto the chair. At first there was just a couple licks of flames and no sound. Then it caught and it started to make a small roar and then some popping and luxurious flames covering it in orange and red lashing tongues of fire. He stood there and felt strangely remote from this situation. He felt this was just one of the practical steps that needed to be taken today and all this week. He felt very capable of making decisions and any emotional outbursts he had yesterday were gone. He was just a witness to the disintegration of what was left of the family he had been raised in.

When he was sure there was not more danger of fire spreading, he hosed the grass around the charred remains of the chair, turned off the water and went into the kitchen to make the coffee. He thought, let's get this goddamn day started.

Laurel

She smelled the smoke before she saw the chair burning. She was not the least bit upset. It was the proper thing to do. She was glad that Simon could do it. She had got dressed after a shower and called the funeral home and asked them to give her a date for the funeral. She had just done all that for her mom, so it did not require much thinking.

She would go to the lawyer in their small town, Ralph Thomas. She knew he had helped her parents with a will several years ago and they needed to get that information straightened out. She did not anticipate any surprises there.

She did have her name on their bank accounts from a visit last year when her mom insisted that be handled now, just in case. Laurel had thought that was premature, considering they weren't even close to 70, but she went along with it because her mom had been so insistent. She knew she would have to go into the bank and meet with a banker, so she called First National and asked for an appointment that afternoon. They would need to pay for a few things right away, like a casket, embalming, interment, etc.

When Simon came in, she was sitting at the kitchen table with her coffee and a piece of toast. She said, "Thank you for handling that chair."

Simon nodded and poured a cup for himself. He could see she had made a list and was already checking things off. He said, "You know, I do not want to stay for too long. The sooner we can get the funeral handled the better. Just keep that in mind when they give you options."

"Well, Simon, I think you are going to help me, aren't you? I mean there are several things we need to do. We can wait for big things, like should we sell this farm and what will happen to Uncle Peter, but I want you to be with me for the other decisions."

Simon gave a half smile and said, "Really Laurel, it cannot be that hard. We just did it. Let's just get him in the ground as quick as we can."

Laurel did not respond. She could feel the tension between them and she did not want to make it worse. She hoped he would stay for the funeral and right now she felt like he could just slip away and not say anything to her, not even good-bye. He was behaving like a child she thought. But, everything considered, she could not really blame him.

Just then her phone rang and it was Newton's Mortuary. They had an opening in two days. Would 10:00 in the morning or 2:00 in the afternoon work best? She started to consult Simon and then just blurted out, 10:00 a.m. is very good. Thank you. Yes, we will be down to pick a coffin. He did like simplicity, so let's look at something wooden and very plain. Yes, we will select flowers. Yes, I will stop in later today and take a look at the choices for a booklet. No, just the same hymns as his wife's and the Lord's Prayer. Thank you.

She hung up and looked at Simon and said, "You can be gone in two days by noon if you want. I'll handle it."

Simon got up from the table and carried his coffee out the back door and let the screen door slam behind him. She called Brenda and said, "Can you pick me up at 11:00? We need to get some things done today."

After she called Brenda, she saw her dad's truck keys hanging on the key hooks by the back door. She realized she could take the truck and do these things by herself. She really did not feel like explaining anything to Brenda about why Simon was not with her or why she was making certain choices. So, she called her back and caught her before she left. She said, "Auntie, I think I am going to go into town using dad's truck if you don't mind. Oh, and maybe you and Uncle Mike could look in on Uncle Peter. I'll go by and talk to him this evening, but I think dad went over there every few days. He will be looking for him. You can tell him whatever you want, but he will know something is wrong when Dad is not there."

Brenda said sure she could do that and yes Mike was planning to head over there this morning. Then she added, "Is Simon going to go with you honey?"

Laurel was quiet for a moment and then she said, with as much control in her voice as possible, even though she wanted to cry, "Well, you know, the DNA test hit him hard. It's just not a good time to try and get him to help with this, so don't worry. I am fully capable of taking care of things today. I'll need your help for the service and the open house afterward."

Brenda felt the gut punch she knew was coming and said, "When the time is right, I can explain what happened. You call me when you want me to come over and do whatever you need me to do. Okay honey? Love you, Laurel."

Laurel hung up and stared straight ahead.

She stood there for a few minutes and then she grabbed her purse and the truck keys and left for town. Just as she started to pull out the driveway, she stopped and turned off the truck.

She walked out to her garden and inspected it. No need to neglect this beautiful garden. She turned on some water and routed it with her hoe down the rows that needed it. She noted it would be time to pull some carrots and pick some cucumbers. She could fill the house with bouquets from the garden. She could dig new potatoes and there were slicing tomatoes ready too. As soon as she was done with the town issues, she would take care of the vegetables and flowers.

Then she remembered the cows and said out loud, "They are going to the sale next Saturday." She called her Uncle Mike on the cell phone and said, "Mike, can you haul the cows to the sale for me Saturday?"

He said sure and offered to milk today. He said, "I'll feed the milk to my pigs unless you want it." She replied quickly, "Go right ahead."

When she pulled into the funeral home she was amazed at how it had not changed since she was a little girl. It was a white building with a peaked roof that was green. The windows were paned with leaded glass on each side of the wide double front doors. There were evergreens planted on each side of the wide steps leading up to the doors and large pedestal pots full of bright summer flowers at the top of the stairs.

When she opened the door the familiar smell of the place hit her. It was musty and floral and heavy. The air conditioning was on high and the carpets were deep plush and a mauve shade. Front and center were the large black walnut doors that opened into the chapel. There was a table beside the doors with leaflets from a funeral that had been held that morning. The business office was to the left and she could see the receptionist sitting there with a large bouquet of lilies on the counter. She knew her name was Mandy from the last funeral they held there; her mom's.

Mandy popped up from her seat and stepped around the counter to greet Laurel. "Mr. Newton is expecting you, Laurel. Please come this way."

This way was two steps and one door into the room that served as a family conference room. It had a long table with plush chairs around it, all in the mauve theme that seemed to permeate the whole place. Mr. Stan Newton, not Bob, was standing at the head of the table and came around to give Laurel the funeral directors warm and lengthy hand shake. His hands were like ice and she almost pulled her hand away immediately.

"Please do sit down Ms. Olsen. We are so sorry to see you so soon after your mother's passing.

We are here to help you in this difficult time."

Laurel sighed and said in a harsher voice than she wanted to use, "Let's just get this done, shall we? I just want you to do basically the same thing you did for my mom. I would like to pick the casket and get on to my other appointments today. Okay?"

"Well, of course, we can go and take a look at those right away. You know we used the silver package with your mother. Are you sure that is the same package you want to use for your father? An upgrade to gold is not very much more."

"Yes, let's stick with the silver thing and I'll be paying with a credit card before I leave."

A few more questions were asked and because she had not sat down during the entire exchange, young Mr. Newton got the hint and they proceeded to the back of the building to a large room full of caskets. Laurel was reminded of how much she hated caskets and the whole idea of burial, but she was here to get this off her list and now was no time to get judgmental. She walked to a cedar casket that was shiny and had red and gold grains in the wood. She said, "This is the one. Please use a dark blue lining and like my mom, close the casket after a brief viewing."

She told him she would drop by with the clothes to dress him in and would have the flowers delivered early on the day of the funeral.

Stan Newton attempted to pat her shoulder and she abruptly stepped away and headed out of the casket room. One more minute in there and she was going to use some choice swear words to describe this whole business of paying huge sums of money to put people in boxes in the ground and let them rot.

She walked back to the counter where Mandy was sitting and said, "I will come back later to pay for everything. I think Stan probably needs to itemize and add up the costs. Thank you."

Before Mandy or Stan could say anything, she was out the door and walking to Rachel's flowers with a stride that was so close to a stomp. She was suddenly filled with anger at her parents. She thought, thank you so much for putting Simon and I in this terrible position of needing to bury you with all your goddamn secrets and very little room for the grief we need to process. Just thank you so much for never talking about anything with us. It is such a pleasure to be all by myself, stomping into to pick flowers for a cheap man who did not believe in spending money on such a stupid thing.

Suddenly she stopped and turned back to the old pick up and hopped in. She would cut flowers early the morning of the funeral and put them in the buckets they used to take flowers to the cemetery on Memorial Day and deliver them to Newton's Mortuary. They could arrange them however they wanted, but she was not going to waste Paul Olsen's money on anymore of this stupidity.

For the first time she laughed and she rolled down the window and put her tanned arm out just like her dad always did and drove over to the lawyer's office.

She pulled up to the small brick building on main street. It had a sign in the window, Law Offices of Ralph Thomas, Esq. Ralph opened the door as she approached and gave her a huge hug. Ralph was a big man and he looked just like he had stepped off a tractor, not stepped out of a posh office. In fact, nothing was posh in his office. There was a very small reception area without any chairs and a short counter with a desk and a picture of an apple orchard in bloom behind it. You could tell an amateur painter had done it, but it was homey and charming all the same. In his actual office he had a nice oak desk, some oak book shelves, but it had a very welcoming feeling and he always sat in one of the three big over-stuffed chairs he had in the office. It felt like you were in his living room.

He had a part time receptionist who was one of his granddaughters, but she was not around today. He locked the front door and said, "I am all yours Laurel."

Laurel smiled at the big friendly man and she felt relaxed for the first time in a week. He offered coffee and she accepted and they settled into the comfortable chairs in his office. He started the conversation. "Well, I suppose we should discuss the will. Your dad made a few changes after your mom passed. Were you aware of that?"

Laurel felt an icy chill go up her back. So much for feeling relaxed. All she could manage to say was, "No."

Ralph pulled his ample body out of his chair and stepped over to his desk and brought back a folder. He looked at her and could see she was distressed. "So, let's just talk in informal language here. Your dad came in about a week after your mom died and asked to change the will. He gave you the farm."

Laurel frowned and said, "Well, too bad. I'm not accepting it. What about Simon?"

Ralph leaned forward and said softly, "He said that the money he has in his private savings can be divided between you." He glanced back at the paperwork and said, "It is sizable, Laurel. Last time he gave me figures it was over $100,000. Also, there is the household savings that both of your parents had and I believe you are included on those accounts. The private savings is to be handled by the Executor, which is you my dear. So, compensation to your brother is going to be easy for you to handle."

Laurel looked at Ralph, looking like a grand-pa and a dad and she thought she could just crawl onto his lap right now and cry like a little girl. She knew he was not to blame for any-thing and she knew this was not simple, but she managed to say, "Thank you Ralph. It is a shock, but it is okay, I guess. I can handle it all. I guess that is what Paul was thinking. Anyway, what bank is this personal savings located at?"

Ralph sighed and said, "First National, just like the other accounts."

"Did my mom know there was another account?"

"I am not sure honey. Her name is not listed on it. I have no idea about that, but it is sizable for a man who had a small farm and did hired hand work. It is impressive to say the least."

Laurel chuckled and let slip, "Oh, my folks were impressive all right. They kept secrets from their kids and from each other and it all is falling on my shoulders now. Very impressive."

Ralph cleared his throat and said, "Let's sign some paperwork and get some needed infor-mation into your hands."

As Laurel drove the old pick up toward home, she began to crumble. She was not ready for the bank experience, so she pulled into a little city park next to the river and let the tears fall. She was so angry. She felt abused and used.

How could both of them leave so much unsaid and frankly undone? So, what if they planned everything out carefully. There were consequences to actions and right now those consequences were hurting their children. Poor Simon, unable to grieve with questions about his whole existence. And now she had this burden of inheritance. More secrets. Secret bank accounts and complexity she thought she would never have to encounter. Her parents were poor in her mind. They never spent money and they never went anywhere. They did not fix up the farm and they just "got by" for some weird reason. Why was her dad stashing all that money? Where did it come from? Did her mom know anything? It was another nightmare, on top of a nightmare, on top of the grief.

When she finally felt she could start up the truck and drive home, she had made up her mind that she was not going to be like them. She was going to spill the whole fiasco and she was going to make Brenda tell them everything she knew. Enough.

Simon

Simon took a lawn chair out into the middle of the orchard. He sat it in the shade and he brought out a small cooler he kept in his trunk. He had some beer in there and it was good beer. It was from one of the local breweries in Bellingham. He popped a can open and took the first delightful cold drinks in gulps.

Did he feel remorseful for abandoning Laurel? Maybe, a little. She did not create this shit show, she just was center stage, the leading lady. He saw his parents now behind a curtain, hidden from view. You could not really see the expressions on their faces and they were far from each other. There was not a thread between them except for Laurel. Poor Laurel, just standing there holding whatever it was that was between them. Was it hate, resentment, ignorance? He was not sure.

He drank another beer, a little slower but still with the intention of getting out of this fucked up head space he found himself in. He had smoked a few joints, but the familiar high seemed to only bring his pain into greater focus, so he thought some alcohol might help. There was whiskey in the house too. He would get to some nice stumbling and hazy place and then pass out on his make shift bedroom in the side yard.

He was thinking about his mom. She was 25 years old when she had him. Such a baby and now he was 33 years old and he realized he had not experienced all that she had gone through as a fairly young woman. He decided to imagine her as a young woman who meets someone and falls in love so fast, even though she has already planned her life with Paul. Whomever his father was he was probably handsome, I mean Simon was always being told how handsome he is, and probably not married or attached in any way. Maybe he was a farm hand. She brought him ice cold lemonade in the orchard and they fell in love. He ravaged her in the tall grass and she returned to meet with him every day for months. For the summer probably before he was born. He was born in June, so the hired hand during the summer made sense. She probably felt sick inside because it was so wrong in her world, but she was crazy in love with this slim dark Italian. Oh, the romance.

Then he switched gears and his father was a low life man who somehow cornered her in the dark barn and raped her. She was so ashamed she could not tell her husband and she told him she needed a break from their intimacy when in fact she was filled with shame and could not bring herself to tell anyone, but of course god-damn Brenda. The keeper of secrets no matter how painfully they would hurt people.

Both stories sounded like cheap romance novels. He did not want either of them to be true. Then he thought, what if I never know? Is that so bad? The man is nowhere to be found and he obviously has not tried to know Simon, so why should he do the work of finding him and giving a damn? Ignorance is bliss.

Not that his time with his step-father, yes let's call him that now, step-father, had been all that great. The man never seemed to like him. He never tried to understand him. But of course, he did not recognize Simon. Why would his son look like he did and act so strange? His simple mind could not get past the differences. There could have been some familiarity, after all he was married to Simon's mother and he knew he had some of her traits. But no, the old man just focused on the differences, like so many people in this place. Different is bad. Do the things that everyone understands. He stood out way too much for this small-minded place.

Another couple beers into his orchard time, he remembered something from a summer picnic that he had completely forgotten. He was about 10 years old and they were having a big celebration, for what he could not remember, but the extended family and friends were coming. Even some cousins from far away and his mom had been cooking for a few days.

They had borrowed two additional picnic tables and he remembered that one was covered in cakes and pies and brownies. Big jars of lemonade were on each table and platters of fried chicken, sliced ham, potato salad, baked beans, fresh vegetables and fruits were displayed on the other two tables. It was a feast and there were lawn chairs and laughter. People were going in and out of the house and the familiar whack of the screen door was heard all day. The sun was hot, but big trees were surrounding the yard and cool little breezes dried the sweat on the faces of the women taking care of the food.

There was a great deal of joy in this picnic. That was the first thing Simon was thinking about and trying to remember that a lot of his childhood was spent in the comfort of family and good food.

The thing that was pulling him into this memory was the fact that his dad asked him to ride with him to pick up Uncle Peter and bring him to the picnic. Peter was a loner and very shy but he did love food and at events like this, putting him a shady spot with a plate of food was a good way to include him. He was family and he needed to be there. That's the way that worked.

When they pulled up to Peter's house, Simon really did not have many memories of his Grandma Gerda living there. She had died before he went to school, so mostly this was Uncle Peter's house. It was already getting overgrown and in between taking care of his own place, Paul tried to get over to rehang a screen door or replace a window. But mostly, it looked like a spooky old house with old climbing roses and ivy clinging to its shabby exterior.

When Peter stepped out of the house, he was looking pretty clean for a change. Simon knew this was because of demands from his mom. She loved Peter but would not tolerate him coming over with stained and smelly clothes. She always washed some things for him and he had on clean jeans and a plaid short-sleeve shirt. His wild hair was combed and he had shaved. Mom would be pleased, Simon thought.

Peter looked at Simon and said, "Diego is here."

Paul shook his head and said, "No, that is not Diego. That is my son, Simon. Now come on Peter, get in the truck. Simon, you ride in the truck bed. Let's go."

Peter said again, "Diego is here."

Paul sighed and said, "Enough of this non-sense. Let's get going so you can eat some fried chicken and fresh green beans. Come on."

Simon remembered the look on Peter's face as he stared at him as he got in the truck. It was a menacing gaze and it was just a little bit scary. After all, Simon was just a little kid and his uncle was weird and "not all there", as his mom always said. As they rode back to their house, he saw that Peter was turning and looking at him as he held on in the back of the truck, dust blowing around his face and hay left in the truck bed flying out the back. Peter was not smiling. He was still looking mean.

Simon remembered that when they got to the house, his mom came out to greet them and when she welcomed Peter, he turned and pointed at Simon and said, "Diego is here." Simon remembered the look on his mom's face, even though it was so long ago, because she never had made that face before. It was a look of terror. She was afraid. She never was afraid of anything that Simon knew of, but somehow this Diego thing was scaring her.

He remembered her whispering to his dad something and he nodded and said, "You know, he has no idea what he is saying. He will forget about it."

Then she came over to me and gave me a hug and said, "Simon, just steer clear of Peter today. He is particularly goofy and you just need to have fun with your cousins and friends. Now run along honey."

For a moment Simon was so locked in the memory that he half expected to turn back to the house and see the yard full of the ghosts of the past, laughing and eating and kids running. But when he did look back the reality of now glared back at him. Just then he heard the old pick up coming down the driveway. He walked down the row of trees, just a bit wobbly from too much beer, and prepared to apologize to his sister.

Brenda

She woke up tired that day. She felt all of her 62 years deep down into her bones. She did not think she had the energy to face what was ahead of her. When Laurel told her she was fine going into handle the funeral herself, she was so relieved. She hoped that Laurel could not tell by the sound of her voice but she probably could. Brenda was too tired to fake it.

After chores, Mike left to go milk Paul's cows and to stop in at Peter's. Before he left, he turned to her and said, "Look Brenda, you do not owe anyone anything. Get rid of these secrets and honey, just remember, you have a beautiful family here. You did not make the same mistakes your sister did. You need to get back to us and let your niece and nephew figure it out. It is theirs to carry, not you." He kissed her on the cheek and said, "I love you honey."

Brenda decided to get the box down from the attic. She had always thought of it as "the box" and she had not opened it for a long time. It was hidden behind some bigger boxes that had old high school yearbooks and scrap books from when she was in school. The bigger boxes were heavy and dusty and she coughed as she pulled them off the low shelf they sat on. There it was; an old cedar box like they had when they were girls. The box had a printed picture that was decoupaged on the top. It was carved and polished and had a small hook clasp that had at one time held a tiny padlock with a little key. These boxes were so popular and you got them and kept your best treasures in them. Their grandma had given them each one. This one had a picture of a thatched cottage on it with flowers and trees surrounding it and a small village painted in the distance.

She blew some of the dust off of it and took it downstairs to her spare bedroom. That room had a desk and she set the box on it. It almost felt like a bomb that needed to be handled with special care. She got a dust cloth and carefully dusted it. The inside of the lid had a mirror and she shined that up too. Then she sat there and spoke to Doris. "I guess it is time to tell your kids the truth. I have put it off for so many reasons. I even fantasized I might never have to tell them anything. But DNA is unlocking family secrets everywhere and your secret is no different. I think Paul went to his grave not knowing that Simon was not his child. I just don't think he could imagine something like that, so he just did not put any clues together. Do you know this was a burden, Doris? I saw Simon suffering as a boy and as a young man, but you never wanted to face up to your reckless behavior and the child it would always impact. You just were selfish like that and I just cannot believe I am saying this out loud, but you were silly and selfish as a young woman. Just stupid really. I mean, you were not really stupid, but you were stupid about how things you did would have long term consequences. You just made one stupid mistake after another. Marrying Paul when you knew he was someone you were just "settling" for. He thought he was marrying the most wonderful girl in the Yakima Valley and you thought you were marrying someone safe and solid. He was that for sure. But there were other options. You were pretty and you had brains and you could have even just gone to Business College in Yakima and met a nice banker or something. But instead, you picked Paul and you were mad at him for the rest of your life. It was not his fault Doris. It was your fault. I do not want to give this box to the kids. I really do not, but now I am forced to. I am 62 years old now and I am tired of carrying my little sister. You asked too much of me."

Brenda felt better. She knew what she had to do and she just felt better. She would explain it to Laurel and Simon, but she was not going to carry the burden of guilt around for the rest of her life. She made her choices and some of them were based on luck, but a lot of them were based on good instincts. She just did not need to keep feeling that somehow, she was part of this mess. She just happened to be a key holder. She was not the creator or owner of this mess. Doris had done that herself.

She called Laurel and was surprised to hear her laughing when she picked up the phone. "Hi, uh, do you want me to come over? I have something for Simon and I want to hear about the plans you have made for the funeral."

Laurel responded, "Sure. No one has started with the casserole deliveries yet, so if you have anything to eat, please bring it. Simon and I are sitting in the yard admiring my garden."

Brenda hung up and headed to the kitchen. She found some lunch meat, bread and cheese. She knew that Laurel had tomatoes and cucumbers and plenty of fresh vegies. She also wrapped up the left-over chocolate cake she had made before Paul died and she grabbed a bottle of wine from the fridge. Good cold Chardonnay. She liked it icy cold and cheap.

She put it all in her basket she used for delivering food and set the time bomb box carefully in the bottom. She was relieved to get that out of her house. She wrote a note to Mike and told him she was not sure how late she would be and if he felt like coming over, please do. Maybe you can tell us what Peter said when you told him. Love you, Brenda.

Laurel

Simon was a little drunk. When she got out of the car with her folder from the lawyer, she saw him staggering a little as he came out of the orchard. He waved and yelled, "Hey! Laurel, I love ya!"

She was in the same better mood that he was in and she smiled and yelled, "Hey! Simon, I love you too!"

When he got to her, he threw his arms around her and said, "I am sorry I have been an ass hole for going on 24 hours now. It's just too much work to be mad at you."

Then she said, "Let's get me caught up to you brother. Follow me." She walked up to the front door and swung it open and yelled, "We are home, your orphan children, and we plan to rock the roof off this place tonight!"

Simon doubled over with laughter and said, "Damn right!"

Brenda

By the time Brenda arrived they were out-side in lawn chairs laughing and eating raw carrots and cucumbers from the garden. They both had a tumbler from the kitchen filled with what looked like whiskey and water. The smoke from their joints was lingering above them and the whole thing was like a funny birthday card. Brenda thought it could have said something like, "Farmer's Cocktail Party" and the inside could say, "Hope your birthday is 'pass out in the yard' fun!"

They both shouted her name when she came around the side yard after dropping the food in the kitchen. "Auntie Brenda, so good you could drop in. Come and join the orphan party. We are drinking our way to stupid!"

From the way they were talking and slurring, she decided she should go in and make some food. She just hugged them both and walked to the garden to pull some more vegetables. She kicked off her shoes and felt the warm dirt between her toes. She grabbed Laurel's market basket that she kept hanging on the fence post by the garden and arranged a basket of fresh vegetables to cut up. She surveyed the garden and thought it looked better than when Doris had taken care of it. She turned and looked at the two of them laughing and talking and she wondered if her sister could see them, somehow, from wherever you went after death. Maybe she could just feel them, but not see them. Maybe she was gone to another place where all that happened on earth was no longer important. But she really believed that love did not die with the person. She must feel love for them.

As Brenda made some sandwiches and arranged the vegetables on a tray, she thought about how good it had felt to be honest with herself about Doris. She had been protecting her all her life and right now that just seemed useless. She did not need protection. She had skipped out on all this and left her to clean it up. But Brenda could do that and she was going to do it tonight.

She was going to call Laurel and Simon in when Mike pulled up. She stepped out to greet him and she saw that he had Peter with him! What a shock. She had not seen Peter in several years. The older he got the more reclusive he became. He looked like a wild man today. His pants were too big and held up with a belt that was so big he had cut off the end of it several times. They were dirty and he had on boots, unlaced, with no socks. His shirt was an old khaki button up that was stained and filthy. His white hair was tangled and shoved under a dirty hat that said, "Farmall" on it. He was looking at the ground and Mike said, "Peter wanted to come and pay his respects to Laurel and Simon."

"Well welcome Peter. Thank you so much for coming. I just made some sandwiches. You can eat with us. Let's eat outside on the picnic table. Mike, can you help me?"

Peter stood there staring at the ground and Simon and Laurel came around the corner. They were drunker than before and they both yelled out, "Uncle Peter! You are here!"

He stepped back but they had each grabbed one of his arms and were leading him into the yard. He shuffled along beside them. Mike looked at Brenda and she mouthed "Drunk as skunks!"

Brenda found a tablecloth in the linen cupboard for the picnic table and she and Mike brought out the food. Peter kept an eye on the food and mostly ignored his niece and nephew who were still talking loudly and laughing. Brenda thought it was time that the two drunks ate some food and settled down.

"Okay everyone. It's time to eat. You must be starved."

Everyone settled down at the table. Eating outside had been suggested for two reasons. One, it was too hard to contain the drunks in the kitchen and two, there was a strong aroma coming off of Peter and it was not pleasant. He was of course oblivious to it and tucked into the food with a great appetite.

Peter looked up from his food after a bit and looked across the table at Simon. He said the famous line from decades ago, "Diego is here." Simon was feeling dangerously confident and he said, "Yes, he is here Uncle Peter. It's me, right? I look just like someone named Diego. Who was he, Uncle Peter, can you tell me because no one else seems to be able to do that?"

Peter said, "Not supposed to say Diego."

Simon answered, "Yeah, I remember that, clear back when I was a kid at a picnic. You got in trouble for saying Diego. But now you can say it over and over again. Diego! Diego! Diego!"

Laurel looked puzzled and said, "What is this about? Who in the fuck is Diego?"

Before anyone else could speak, Simon said,

"I believe he is my dad. Anyway, he is a big secret and now we can talk about it. Right, Brenda?"

Brenda looked straight ahead and she said in a clear voice, "Yep. We can all talk about it now. Excuse me a moment."

She returned to the table with the wooden box from her attic. She handed it to Simon and said, "Answers are in here and I can fill in all the blanks."

Mike chimed in too, "I know most of it too, so I'm as guilty as your aunt for keeping things a secret. We just thought it would be too much for your dad and unfortunately, your mom thought so too."

Brenda rested her head on Mike's shoulder and mouthed, "Thank you."

Simon and Laurel sobered up quickly. Peter dove into a piece of chocolate cake, still focused on the food. The box was opened.

On top was a letter, written in the familiar hand writing of Doris. It was not too long and was written on one side of lined notebook paper. Underneath it there were some photos and a watch, a locket, and a knife in a leather pouch.

Laurel took the letter and said, "Shall I? Because next I am going to be reading the will to you all. Let's get things out in the open."

Simon nodded and Laurel read the following letter:

Dear Children;

I am writing to let you know that things have not always been what they seemed in our family. I am asking for your forgiveness first because I was young, stupid and incapable of hurting your father.

In the summer of the year before I turned 25 years old, I fell in love with a man named Diego Lombardi. He came to the Yakima Valley to survey farms and complete and irrigation study for the University of Washington. He was my age and he had come to America to study. He was from Italy.

When we met, he and I hit it off and we spent a lot of time talking and laughing in the kitchen. Your dad was working all the time and I was lonely. Things got out of hand and we ended up having a secret relationship, at night, in his car, away from the farm.

During that time, I could not have an intimate relationship with your father. Guilt. So, when I discovered I was pregnant, I knew Diego was the father.

He was already gone and although we intended to write and try to stay in touch we never did. I was just another conquest and he was young, free and from a wealthy family. I was married, had a 3-year-old and was not going anywhere.

So, that is it. Not too romantic and not too

exciting, but at the time I was with Diego, I truly was in love and infatuated with his differences and just plain stupid.

Diego does not know you exist, Simon. Your father never was told about Diego. I am sorry that I left out this important part of your life out of embarrassment and selfishness. I love you dearly. You do resemble him very much as you can see from the enclosed picture. That picture is from an article in the Seattle Times that he shared with me.

Your mother,
Doris Olsen

Simon laughed out loud. "Seriously, was that so hard. Jesus, I think everyone could have handled that information. Jesus, and I just cannot believe Dad did not know; he treated me like an interloper my whole life. Good God, Mom, this is pathetic."

Brenda spoke up, again with a clear tone, like the rehearsals she had performed in her mind a million times. "Simon, you would have to have been an adult in those times to understand this situation. If anyone would have found out your mom would have really suffered and so would have your dad. Your mom was trying to handle things so that no one suffered, but her. She suffered for the rest of her life. She understates how much she fell for

Diego and how much it hurt when he never got in touch with her again. And she suffered because it was the way she probably should have gone in life; left this valley, left the farm and made something else of her life. She just was afraid and she could not do it."

Then Mike said, "Your mom was just working with what she had and that was the life that was already started; marriage and children and the farm life."

Laurel said, "Well, she always tried to protect you from everything Simon, you know that. She was always sticking up for you, covering your tracks. She must have just been filled with guilt. Jesus..."

Simon took out the article that she had laminated and there was Diego and he did look just like him. Diego had longer hair too and there was the nose and the shape of the mouth and he was thin, like a rail. The other picture was of his mom. She was standing on the back porch, apron and house dress, her hair long then and dark. She was laughing and had her hands on her hips. Her feet were bare and you could just see Laurel peaking around her skirt. She was beautiful, exquisite, and he had never seen this picture before. On the back in an unknown handwriting it said, "Bella Doris, Summer, 1978". Diego had captured a look he did not think he had ever seen on his mother's face. It was sexual and carefree and very flirtatious. He handed it to Laurel.

Then he picked up the watch. It was old. He thought it looked like a military watch. The brand was Raid and it had a skull and cross bones with the years 1936–1939 under it. The face was dark brown with white lettering, half in roman numerals and half in numbers. The band was dark leather and it appeared to be in great shape. There was no note or explanation attached.

The locket was one he had seen his mom wear a few times and when he opened it there was a picture of Diego and a picture of him, cut small with just their heads showing. It was heart shaped and it was gold. Again, no note or explanation.

Finally, there was a pocket-sized knife that folded and had a horn handle, pearly in color. It was inside a small leather pouch. It did have a note inside the pouch. It read; "All three of these things came from Diego. He gave them to me when he was here. He came from wealth and he was not really attached to material things like you might think. The watch and locket are valuable."

Simon shut the box and looked around the table at what was left of his family. He did not know what he was supposed to say or do right now. He was jumbled up and suddenly way too sober. Laurel broke the silence.

"Well, that was a lot. But we are not done. I

have some news to share about the will and since we all feel less than great, let's just get it out now. No 'Olsen style' holding it in, okay?"

She picked up a folder that she had sitting beside her on the table and she said, "Dad changed his will. He left the farm to me. He had a secret bank account of over $100,000 and I am supposed to split that with Simon, along with the other money they have left in their joint savings and checking. I didn't go to the bank today to check out figures because this was a little too much for me to digest. And before anyone can say anything, I have no intention of cutting my brother out of any inheritance. If I sell the farm, he gets half. If I keep the farm, he gets half of the value. I have no idea why Dad did this, but it's ridiculous and that's that."

Simon laughed out loud and said, "Well what about poor fucking Peter here? What is he supposed to do? And I don't want that old man's money or anything to do with this farm. I mean, come on, he is not my dad."

Laurel looked sideways at Simon and said, "Well, I'm not going to do what he wanted. I think there is provisions for Peter, I just did not read any of it. Ralph just gave it to me straight, like Ralph always does."

Brenda and Mike sat there and you could see they were stunned. Mike looked over at

Peter and he had heard his name more than once, so he was looking back and forth between all of them with a panic on his face. "Hey, Peter, you are just fine buddy. You do not have to worry. We will all make sure you stay right in your house for as long as possible. You are safe, Paul made sure of that."

Peter nodded at Mike and asked for more lemonade. Brenda sat there looking like she had aged 10 years in an hour. Simon was staring at the box and Laurel had her head in her hands. Who knew what was going to happen next? It felt like the worst had already happened, but life is full of surprises. There would be more to come.

Laurel

The funeral came and went. Her favorite part of the day was delivering the flowers to The Newton Mortuary, freshly picked from her garden. Apparently, Stan had been promoted to full time mortician and he was a little rattled by the buckets of fresh garden flowers and boughs of thorny climbing roses. As he started to express his concerns, Laurel turned to him and said, "Thank you so much for your kindness, Stan. The family really appreciates it. I'll see you at 10!" Laurel left him standing there, confused and nodding his head and she breezed out the front door.

The rest was the same drudgery and emotions as when her mom had passed. Of course, there was the good feelings she had for all the people who showed up to pay their re-spects. She smiled as so many said they had never seen such beautiful flowers at a funer-al. She was glad to see that Mandy must have stepped in and helped Stan and maybe even his wife. They were arranged in a multitude of vases and the roses were spread across the casket, looking very much in place. She knew her dad would be so happy about that and he was a good hard-working man after all, with his flaws, but with his good strong heart.

Simon chose to stay a little longer than he had originally planned. He wanted to help Laurel with a few things and he knew she had a lot more to think about than he did. He could leave and go home and this was her home and now she had some big life decisions to make. He was very clear with her that he did not think she needed to make any decisions just yet. "Take your time, sis. Take care of the garden and the chickens and think about what you really want to do. Do not rush."

Laurel knew he was right and she had re-alized she was not ready to just sell the farm and go. Go where? She had no desire to go anywhere right now.

Simon accompanied her to the bank and they were both surprised at the amount of money that had been left to them. There was

$150,000 in the "secret" account of Paul's. There was $100,000 in the joint savings and $50,000 in the joint checking. They decided to split it and move it into their own separate accounts. They could figure out next steps for the money later.

Laurel also found the deed to Uncle Peter's place and it was now also willed to her. They also found an account that was managed for Peter by Paul and one of his other brothers. It had regular deposits of $1000 per month and it had grown to a sizeable account as Peter did not require very much. Laurel would get in touch with her Uncle Karl to discuss that situation.

She reiterated to Simon many times over that either she would be buying him out on the farm or they would sell it and split the money. Simon just shook his head and said, "Really, I do not need that money or want it, but whatever floats your boat, Laurel."

They both noticed that Brenda was avoiding them. She was not there peering into the paperwork or asking questions about what they planned to do. She had just faded out for now and they realized they were happy about that. It was just the two of them and it felt good. They were healing.

Simon helped her pack up their parent's clothes and take them to Good Will. She kept a couple of her mom's dresses and one of her dad's shirts. Simon wanted one of their mom's brooches that she had been given from her grandmother. It was real gold with pearls and looked like a bunch of flowers. It was very elegant and he had no idea who he would ever give it to, but he wanted to keep it for himself.

They cleaned the house thoroughly and took down things they both thought were too old or too ugly. Simon scrubbed all the floors and Laurel shampooed the few carpets. They moved things out of the stuffy room that Simon had to sleep in and created a nice guest room in the sewing room downstairs. Neither of them wanted the sewing machine and decided they would ask Brenda if one of her girls wanted it.

They did not touch the barn or the shed, but they did paint the front porch with fresh white paint. They hung new curtains in the kitchen as the old apple pattern had faded and yellowed. They chose bright blue gingham and it just lit up the room.

They worked hard for two weeks and the whole time they laughed and cried and talked and worked some more. Laurel had never seen Simon dive in the way he was physically. It made her sad that he had always held back for fear of being ridiculed by Paul. She knew he would be saying rude things if he saw Simon had ironed the new curtains and hung them.

He would have said, "What about the barn and the shed? He needs to help you out there too."

But she watched Simon closely and could see he was adjusting to his new found heritage. He was not curious and did not talk about finding Diego Lombardi. He felt that it was a useless pursuit. He had no interest in the other half sister and he never did receive any correspondence or attempt from her to meet him. She must have felt abandoned too. Or maybe she grew up with the Romeo, he just did not care.

Simon was sensitive and the fact that his paternity had come to light and caused him so much turmoil made him leery of doing that to someone else. Diego would be hurt and angry with himself. The half–sister was an unknown. How many people probably had half siblings they never met? It was better to just stay out of the extended drama that trying to reach either of them would cause.

On the last day Simon was planning to be there, they spent the day in the yard, lounging and drinking wine and admiring the property. It seemed more beautiful to them both and for the first time that Laurel could ever remember her brother said, "I should move in here with you Laurel. I think I could work remotely. I mean look at this oasis."

She looked at him in amazement and said, "Are you serious?"

Simon chuckled and said, "I don't think so. I just had a good time here without the pressure of dad and frankly, Brenda. Just taking in all that is good about this place, it felt so right. Anyway, there is plenty of time to think about doing something that crazy!"

Laurel smiled and said, "If you want to, I'll stay right here and live with you. We are both the non-marrying type."

Then they talked about the amount of money their dad had kept in a secret account and they guessed he probably put money in there from work on his other farms. Maybe some of it he inherited from Grandma Gerda. He always acted like he was down to his last penny and he hated spending money on anything. Simon thought maybe he had nothing to spend it on. He never thought they needed anything new. The beds were the original mattresses from when they got married. He bought a new one for the sewing room. He was going to be comfortable any time he stayed here.

Laurel kept going back to the way her mom had planned her funeral, even picking out her headstone. Where did she get the money for all of it and who does that at 58 years old? She was really not quite ready to dig into that, but she was going to. Sure enough, it happened before Simon left.

Both she and Simon were angry at Brenda

and they let themselves talk about that too. They understood it to a degree, but they also felt like she was the older sibling and she should have told their mom that Simon deserved to know and so did Paul. The more they talked and thought about their dad they were very certain he did not know anything about Simon being Diego's son. He would have burst out at some point, someday, somehow, and screamed at Doris and at Simon. But that did not happen. He was, as Laurel had said, a simple man.

One thing they did do during those two weeks was look into the value of the watch and the locket. The watch was worth $19,000. It was Italian and it was a military watch. The locket was 18 carat gold and was worth $4,500. It was astounding. Laurel thought he should hang onto them, but he was already thinking about calling an antique auction house. They meant nothing to him. He said, he would keep the pocket knife. He liked it.

Thus, the Olsen children pulled things to-gether in the summer of 2012. They had been through a lot of change in only 4 short months. They now needed some normalcy and time to reflect.

Angela & Carrie

(The Cousins)

Angela was 40 and Carrie was 38. They were well thought of in their small town. Smart, pretty, married local boys, had multiple children, worked only part time and only when their children were in school. They lived close to each other on the edge of town in newer houses in the newer neighborhoods that had popped up as people were starting to move to their small town from Yakima, the medium size city. It was a quick commute with the new highway.

Angela was the oldest of the four cousins and she always took her role very seriously. When they were all little she looked out for her sister and Aunt Doris' two kids. She was not really the farming type of girl and she had instead gone into hair styling and cosmetology and worked several days a week for a shop in town. She was a pretty woman with blonde (dyed) hair and her mother's blue eyes. She had three daughters and she took excellent care of them. She knew all their friends and all their friends' mothers and she tracked their school performance diligently. Angela was the consummate small-town girl and she was very comfortable with herself.

Carrie was only two years younger and she also married a local boy. His parents had been the wealthiest people in their small town, owning a large farm and other properties. Her husband took over the family business and he suggested she could work or not work; they would have enough to raise their two boys. Carrie liked working and she could not wait for both of the boys to be in school and she started working in Yakima in the office at one of the large fruit warehouse companies, of course part time. She enjoyed dressing up for the office and having a separate life of work. She wore her auburn hair long and dressed in the latest fashions.

She was not the consummate small-town girl, but she was happy with what she had. Her boys were a bit rowdy, long legged, rough housers and spent hours with their dad in the big orchards he was in charge of and that suited her just fine. More time to spend at home, decorating and shopping in Yakima. She loved them but really did not completely understand them.

The two sisters were both musicians and Carrie had a nice singing voice. Angela played the harp. They did weddings and funerals often and they started charging for their services when they got in their 30's. It took time and they had to learn the latest favorite wedding and funeral songs (which do not change much) and plus, good to make a little side money.

The sisters were sitting in Carrie's kitchen about a week after Uncle Paul's funeral. Their conversation went to a familiar place; resentment regarding Aunt Doris and her weird children. Oh, and of course, their own mother's obsession with all of them.

They were having ice tea and salad and sitting at the kitchen island. The house was beautifully decorated, tasteful and Carrie did not have one bit of the "country look" going on like her friends. She liked clean lines, earth tones, a picture that could speak for a whole room, new dishes and glasses that reflected her very sophisticated taste. The setting looked like they could have been posing in a decorator's magazine.

Angela said, "Can you believe that Mom is not over at Laurel's place constantly? I mean, she probably told them about Aunt Doris' illness and now they hate her or something. How that could remain a secret was just a fairy tale."

Carrie pointed her fork at Angela and said, "I agree. I mean, why did Mom always protect Doris so much? Anyway, poor old Paul, he just thinks his wife dropped dead on their bedroom floor. Cripes, Doris just treated him terribly. He was always such a nice old Uncle."

Angela nodded and added, "Well, their kids turned out weird. I mean, neither of them is married, they never come and see us and it's like, so what, Laurel moved back, she is no-where to be seen."

Carrie added, "Yes. She gets in touch with her old gal pals from high school and once she hears they are as messed up as her, she just disappears again. I mean Maria said she was so weird. Big surprise."

Angela said, "She was normal enough in school, but Simon was the one no one could imagine coming from that family. All that walking and his long hair when it was not cool and the way he followed Laurel around when we were kids, creepy."

This chat when on for a while, much hashed over material from other conversations they had engaged in for years. Then Angela said, "Do you think that Laurel and Simon know about the times Doris was admitted to the psych ward? Remember when they would stay with us and were told their mom was in Seattle visiting her friend Patricia? I have never ever heard them say anything about that."

"Yeah, they were only little, right? I mean, we didn't even know until we were older. It might be good if they knew, you know, cuz God knows if they suffer from any of her weird ailments."

"Mom probably won't tell them. Always protecting Doris... I don't think I could lie to your kids, Carrie, I mean for years. Just don't ask me too! Of course, you are squared away."

Carrie laughed and said, "Well, both of us are good. Whatever weird ass genes Aunt Doris got, passed us by. Seems like Mom didn't get them either. Did you hear that they have been fixing up Uncle Paul's house? I wonder if that means they are selling it."

Angela shook her head and said, "When Laurel moved in, Mom said she left everything in Seattle behind her, so she has nowhere else to go, unless she moved to weird Bellingham and hung out with her queer brother."

"Oh Angela, stop it! Plus, you don't even say 'queer' anymore. I think you are supposed to say gay. Well, I could care less what they do. Obviously, they are not interested in hanging out with us and our families. They must just hate kids!"

This conversation went on for a while and then it was time for both of them to get back to their Saturday chores. When they parted Angela hugged Carrie and said, "You are the best sis. Talk to you tomorrow."

Carrie answered, "Right back at ya!"

Brenda

Brenda was seriously considering going to a counselor. She had never done anything like that in her life. She was not even sure who she should call and she was not sure she felt good about anyone but Mike knowing about it. She was just not having such a good time right now.

She had been staying home a lot. There was harvesting of the garden and peaches and pears to can, but she knew she was using that as an excuse. She was not going for coffee with any of the other women she usually kept in touch with and she was completely avoiding bothering Doris' kids.

In fact, she knew that all of her involvement with them since their mom had died needed to come to an end. She had helped them as much as she could, but frankly, she did not understand them.

There was still the information left unshared about how their mom had taken her own life. They had no idea that she had been filled with cancer and had procured enough "medicine" to end it all. They had no idea that the plan was for her to stay in the bed and just let Paul think it was a heart attack. Doris knew he would call the funeral home and she was not concerned with anyone finding out, of course except Brenda knew and so then did Mike. He was her husband and they kept no secrets.

How come she ended up face down on the bedroom floor? Brenda tried to chase away the thought that maybe she had changed her mind and was trying to get to the bathroom. Maybe she decided she wanted to try and live so she could say good-bye to Paul and the kids. But there was no way of knowing why.

Brenda cried and agonized all of the days before Doris died. She told Mike they had to intervene and when he said, okay, she lashed out and said, she gets to choose. Yes, she gets to choose. Had it been a horrible thing to do, to ask your only sister to lie for you? Well, yes, but Brenda had always said yes to anything Doris wanted to do. This would be no different.

Brenda was thinking that it was probably

unnecessary to tell them now. How would she explain letting her sister gather up the poison and agreeing to stay silent? What would they gain from it? Maybe, medical history, but really, didn't every family have dozens of people who died of cancer in their history?

She thought about when Dr. Timothy from Yakima had called her sister one last time to discuss treatment options. She had been there that afternoon and she heard Doris tell him, "I have decided against treatment. I am going to let this cancer take its course. No thank you, I don't want hospice. I know it will be painful, yes, I will probably reconsider when it gets that way. Thank you for everything Dr. Timothy. Yes, thank you."

She had turned and looked at Brenda and said, "I am going to get some poison and I am going out without anyone else having to suffer. Paul will do better with a sudden death. Long drawn-out deaths are not something he can do. Remember his mom? That was horrible."

Brenda remembered saying, "But what about Laurel and Simon? Don't they deserve to know something?"

Doris sat down at the table and said, "No. They will want me to try and they will want to hover and I just want to go before all of that happens. You have got to help me, Brenda. I just cannot do that to any of them."

Brenda wanted to scream, "But what about me?" Of course, she did not scream or make a big dramatic show and beg her to reconsider. She knew Doris. It would be just like everything else in her life; she was doing it her way even if it was wrong.

Brenda thought about whether it was wrong. She tried to put herself in Doris' shoes and no matter what, she knew she would fight for more time with her family. She saw those beautiful grandchildren in her mind and every birthday, graduation, wedding, all of it, she wanted to be present. That is what she would fight for. She would fight for Mike and being with him for every greedy second she could pull out of this life. She would have done it for Doris too, just to spend time with her and laugh and remember all the good things.

But Doris wanted out. As much as she loved Laurel and Simon, they were separate from her now. They did not need her. They did not spend much time around her. Paul was Paul and she felt for him but she knew he would basically not change his routine. She knew Laurel and she thought she would choose to help her dad for as long as she could stand it. After all, for all her success and education she seemed to be unhappy. Simon was always going to struggle.

Brenda thought about the finances some

and she too was puzzled by Paul's ability to save so much, but, thank God, it really was not her business. She could just forget about it now. So what? Doris did not have nice things she could have had, but Doris was always in the process of punishing herself for past decisions. She would never have been comfortable with too many nice things.

On the afternoon before Simon was planning to drive back to Bellingham, she drove over to check on the progress of the cleanup. When she pulled in the driveway, she laughed out loud when she saw Paul's truck pulled up on the lawn and being washed by Simon. Paul only hosed it off every few months, she was sure.

It took her back to the time that Paul bought that truck. It was a big deal for him to buy something new, right off the lot. He was 18 years old at the time and he and Brenda had just graduated from high school. He had been working and earning money since he was 12 years old. It was rumored he paid cash for it. It was two tone beige and brown and at first, he kept it in great shape inside and out. As the years went by and he used it for farm work it became a little shabbier looking of course. But he kept it in perfect running shape and had decided it was a lifetime purchase. That was Paul for you.

Simon looked up when she pulled in and gave her a half wave, as she would describe it. Not a welcoming wave, like so glad you stopped in, but a wave of acknowledgement, like, oh it's you.

She stepped out of her car and found herself groaning as she straightened up. Damn old body. Laurel stepped out of the house wearing a pair of overalls and holding a couple of beers in her hand. "Hello Aunt Brenda. How are you doing?"

Brenda smiled and said, "Okay, honey. Looks like you two are taking care of things nicely."

Laurel nodded and said, "Simon stayed to help me. We have had some fun too. It's hard and all but it feels good. Come on in."

Brenda said, "I'll just take a quick peek at the inside and then I have some errands to do." She did not have any errands. Mike had been handling all that for her.

She marveled at how clean the inside of the house looked. It smelled good and fresh and she loved the new curtains in the kitchen. The floors were shiny and the windows were open with cross breezes cooling the entire house. She looked in the old sewing room and admired how bright it was and the new bed and the new rug.

Laurel said, "Would you or your girls want this sewing machine? Neither of us want it."

Brenda did not want it nor did her girls, but she found herself saying, "Sure. Thanks so much. I'll take it with me today."

Then Laurel said, "Is there anything you want of Mom's?"

Brenda thought about that for a moment. When she finally spoke, her voice was a little shaky. "Actually, she gave me a few things this spring. I think everything else should stay with you kids."

Laurel sighed and said, "Aunt Brenda, are you ever going to tell us what happened to Mom? She did not just die and we both know it. Can you please just tell us? Was it cancer? Was it some other weird disease?"

Brenda looked at the floor and her shoulders started to shake. Laurel walked her into the kitchen and sat her down in a chair. She poured some coffee and put a shot of whiskey in it and sat it in front of Brenda. Then she sat down beside her and put her arm around her shoulders. She said, "Mom asked too much of you Auntie. She was selfish like that."

Brenda broke right then. The tears flooded out of her and she sobbed in great gulps. She lost all sense of trying to hold it in and she just let it all flood out of her like a tsunami. She laid her head in her hands and Laurel brought a box of tissues over and handed her one after another.

Laurel was good like that. She was calm. She had always been that way. Brenda leaned on her shoulder now and finally could say, "I am so sorry Laurel."

Just then Simon walked in the back door. He took in the scene and grabbed a cold beer out of the fridge and sat down across from the two women. When he popped the top, Brenda looked up and wiped her eyes. She said, "I am sorry Simon."

Simon smiled at her and said, "No need to be sorry Aunt Brenda. Our Mom should be sorry. But she is not here to say that. So, stop carrying her on your back Auntie."

He took a long drink of his beer and then said to Laurel, "So, what did Mom die of?"

Laurel shook her head at him and said, "I'll take one of those cold beers too."

Doris/Brenda

No one could explain what happened to Doris better than Doris herself. You may not believe in life after death. You may not believe in someone returning from death and communicating through another person. Believing it or not believing it is not required. This is what happened in the Olsen kitchen on a late summer day with the sun shining through the new blue gingham curtains and the stacks of fresh vegetables on the drain board.

Doris chose Brenda as her communicator. When Laurel and Simon discussed the experience later, they both remembered it the same and it started with Brenda sitting straight up and not crying anymore. They also remembered that the room seemed strangely lit, like there was a light fog all around them. They experienced it and therefore they did not doubt it happened. Brenda shared that she could hear her sister speaking through her, but she could not control it or stop it. It happened quickly.

Brenda's voice took on a huskier tone, which was how Doris sounded. She had smoked into her 40's and you could hear it in her voice. Now Brenda was sounding just like her. She (Doris or Brenda, take your pick) said, "I want you both to know how much I love you. I wanted to stay with you and I did not want to leave the world yet. I wanted to be there for your dad too. He needed me. I wanted to stay for my wonderful sister Brenda too. I wanted the world to stop and let me stay. But cancer got me. Please forgive me and forgive your aunt. She did not approve of what I did, but she never turned her back on me. Your dad never knew. You need to listen to me because it was all my decision. I left quickly to save everyone and myself the pain and agony of the death I was facing. You need to find a way to be at peace with it if you can."

Then she was gone. As quickly as her voice appeared, it left. Brenda shook her head and said in her own voice, "What was that?"

Simon stared at Brenda and Laurel and said, "It was Mom."

Laurel nodded her head, yes, and she reached across the table to grab Simon's hand. "That just happened. We all heard her. That was real."

"Yeah, it happened. That just happened, right here, right in the kitchen." Simon sounded resolved that it was in fact their mom.

Brenda spoke so softly, "It was pancreatic cancer. They told her in March she had 3 months. It was so fast, the only symptoms she had were tummy aches and she had always had a weak stomach. When she started to have more pain, she went to Dr. Timothy and he did a couple tests and that was it."

Simon asked, "But how did she do it? I mean do they just let you do that and not tell anyone?"

Brenda sighed and said, "I am not 100% sure how she got the drugs. I do not think it was legally done. She told me the less I knew the better. She went to Yakima alone several times and she came back and told me the date and time. It was fast and confusing and I just did not have the heart to stop her. She made up her mind, completely."

"I just don't understand how she could get a lethal dose of something. I mean, it's just crazy. Who did she know that could help her get it? I mean, what the fuck was it?" Simon got up and paced around the kitchen.

Brenda looked wiped out and Laurel said,

"Simon, you drive Auntie home and I will follow you. She is exhausted. I think whatever just happened zapped her."

Simon helped Brenda out of her chair and walked her to her car. He threw his keys at Laurel and said, "Pick me up at her house."

That's how they left it that day.

Laurel

Simon stayed for a few more days. It felt better to be together for a while. The experience, or as they began referring to it, "the reveal" had been strange. The information that she had cancer was not the shocking part. They had been thinking that for a long time. The information that she took her own life using some ill-gotten drugs, a little more surprising. That she did that to her sister, making her vow to keep it secret, pretty selfish, but after everything else they were learning about their mom, not totally unbelievable.

No, it was the realization that she had come back to tell them. Neither of them doubted it for one second and neither of them thought they would tell anyone. It was so personal and so out of the realm of normal that they just decided that it was their gift from their mom and no one needed to know and conjecture how bizarre they were becoming.

Laurel rang Brenda first thing to let her know Simon was planning to stay a little longer and then she said, with great respect, "Aunt Brenda, we are not planning on sharing any of what we heard yesterday with anyone. We are not going to talk about how we found out either, so, please, if you can just keep it between you and Uncle Mike, we would really appreciate it."

"Oh, yes, of course honey, it will never go beyond that. It was so, well, intimate I guess is a good word. It was for you and Simon. I will never reveal any of it. I love you both so much and I loved your mom, even with her many issues and secrets." Brenda sounded good and calm, if not still tired.

Laurel turned to Simon after she hung up and said, "What a relief for Aunt Brenda. I mean, seriously, I cannot imagine how she handled it. She is much tougher than I thought she was."

Simon was making a good breakfast for them and he checked the waffle iron before saying, "I think she only did it for love. What else could it be for?"

Laurel nodded her head and poured some more coffee. She had brought in the nice coffee maker her dad and mom would not use and put the old percolator in the shed, on a shelf. She put her dad's favorite coffee mug beside it and his cap he wore to work. It was a small shrine, and she could not bear to throw any of it out.

She looked around the kitchen and admired the beautiful Norwegian side board. She had polished it up and the Rosemaling was looking brighter. She had rubbed out most of the scratches. She would never part with it.

She looked at the dishes she grew up eating on; white and blue stoneware. They were Pfaltzgraff, the Yorktowne pattern. They were very nice and her mom had used them for every day. She got them when they got married and they were one of the few things she took great pride in owning. Laurel had given her many pieces throughout the years from yard sales and thrift stores. There was a good selection of all pieces now. Laurel loved the heft of them and the smooth whitish gray surface, with the distinctive blue flowers in the center. She always kept a small bud vase from that set on her bedside table, sticking a lone rose or even a flowering weed (that was in the alley ways of Seattle) in it. These would stay with her too. Simon could make a second set with all that they had if he wanted, but that could be decided later.

The house was becoming a representation of herself and of Simon, with the sentimental touches from her mom and dad. She realized just at that moment that she was not going to leave. She did not have everything figured out, but she was staying. That was the one thing that was absolutely clear for her. This is where she belonged. This was where she was her true self. And it belonged to her now.

Simon was serving up the waffles with the sliced peaches and crispy bacon on the side. He sat down across from her and when he looked at her, he said, "What? You have a look, what is it?"

She smiled and said, "I am going to live her now Simon. I mean, forever I think."

Simon looked at her and his mind went back to the first day he found out she was leaving Seattle behind and planning to stay with their dad. That seemed like 100 years ago and it was only 4 short months ago. He had been shocked and disgusted at the news. He thought it was short sighted and frankly ridiculous. He thought it was a grief thing and could not understand why she did not just take a leave of absence from work. The thought of living in the hot and dry Yakima Valley with a crabby old man just did not seem like a sound decision.

Now when he looked at her, he saw a version

he did not know was quietly waiting to come forward. She had never been as beautiful as she looked right now. Her auburn hair had taken on a new shine from all of the sunshine. She was tanned and her blue eyes stood out more than he could ever remember. She was at home in the clothes she wore each day and she moved with a different grace than when he had visited her in the city. There she had seemed uncomfortable and he frankly worried about her mental state. He had no reason to worry now.

"Well, sister of mine, I am so happy for you. You are in the world you belong in now. You are 100% Laurel." He moved his coffee cup to hers in a toast and said, "To my beautiful sister farmer!"

Laurel smiled and said, "I plan to go to a realtor and find out what the value of this property is and you will be getting half of that as soon as I can arrange it. I probably will have to take out a loan, but that is not a problem. I will not leave you out."

Simon laughed. "Hold on now, don't take out any loans. Remember, I said, think about things for a while. You always want to check off your list. Put that away for now and just think about your everyday life here. I have enough of my own savings and money and I am not eager to have anymore. Just slow down and enjoy your decision."

Laurel knew he was right about that. She was task focused and that task could wait. For now, she had a few other things to think about and they were more pressing. She had already started the list and it was in her drawer in her bedside table.

Then Simon asked her, "Do you need to know what poison mom used and where she got it?"

Laurel laughed now and said, "I could give a flying fuck Simon! She took her life and she had a good reason and I am not curious about any details. Are you?"

"Nope. Let it lie, I say." Simon started clearing the table and when he looked out the window over the kitchen sink, he said, "Life is just so unpredictable. I have a load of things to think about myself."

Laurel looked at his back, tall thin and beautiful man. His hair always shone with that blue black color. She loved him so much and she was so grateful to have him. She even thought, "I am glad he is Diego's son. I probably would have not enjoyed Paul's son."

Brenda

It was about one week after the "reveal" that Brenda called her daughters and said she would like to fix them lunch very soon and could they figure out a time to come and visit. She did this periodically because she enjoyed seeing them and their lives were so busy, she had to get on their schedules.

A date was set for the next week on Tuesday at 11:30 a.m. Both girls had that day off and arranged to come over to their mom's house. Carrie brought some fresh zinnias from her yard and Angela baked some chocolate chip cookies. When they arrived, there was their sweet mom in her yellow apron and her hair pulled up in a nice bun. She had on a nice pair of pressed jeans and a pink striped blouse. She had on a pair of pearl earrings. She had taken some time getting ready. She even had on blush and lipstick.

"Hello Mom! You look great!" Carrie put the bouquet of zinnias on the kitchen table and helped herself to a cold glass of ice tea.

Angela hugged her mom hard and said, "You look so much better than you did a couple weeks ago. I am so happy to see you."

They all settled in for a nice leisurely lunch with homemade quiche and crispy garden-fresh vegetables. The girls caught their mother up on all the latest things their children were up to. The school year was underway and there were clubs and after school sports and all manner of things that they were involved in. Brenda thought they were probably keeping their kids too busy, but that was the way things are now. Nobody meets the kids at the door with homemade goodies and then they run outside to play and explore. No, here's a packaged snack and get changed for soccer, basketball, dance, gymnastics, football, baseball, something!

She never mentioned how she felt about it to the girls because she really did not think she needed to be involved. They were from a different generation than her and she was happy to be standing by watching.

She finally got around to the real reason

she had invited them. She started out by saying, "Well, I told Laurel and Simon about their mom's illness and how she took her own life."

Carrie exclaimed, "Oh good Mom. How did they take it?"

Angela chimed in, "Yes, were they furious with her or you or what?"

Brenda wanted to be careful with her words because she had promised Laurel that she had not told anyone but Mike and she felt badly about lying. She also remembered she should not tell them anything about the "reveal" and she told herself; I just won't talk about that.

"Well," she said, "they took it very well. They both had been suspicious all along. They were kind to me and understanding and they did not say anything about being angry with their mom. I think they handled it very well."

"Wow," said Angela and Carrie at the same time.

Carrie said, "Even Simon? I mean he is the more emotional of the two, being gay and all. I thought he might really fall apart."

"Well, he did not. He is a very nice person and very strong. Everyone who is gay is not overly emotional." Brenda felt defensive.

"Yeah," said Carrie. "But remember he has always been so weird and I don't know, out of place. I guess I don't know him very well or something."

"Well, you don't know him very well and whose fault is that, Carrie?" Brenda had a real edge in her voice.

Angela said, "Mom, stop. You always stick up for those guys. We think they are weird and that is all there is to it. I mean no relationships, no marriages, practically as reclusive as their Uncle Peter. And what about their mom's suicide and you being forced to keep that secret? Were they apologetic?"

"Yes, they were apologetic. That is for sure. They understood what it was doing to me. But then when Doris told them in her own words..." Brenda clapped her hand over her mouth and said, "Shit."

Carrie said, "What in the hell are you talking about? Doris told them? When?"

Both girls looked at their mom and saw that she had turned bright red and was fumbling with her ice tea glass. Angela said, "Please explain Mom. You are not making sense."

Brenda did not feel strong in the face of her daughters. If the truth was known they had been in charge for a long time. They both were strong and had been born into a totally different time than their mom and dad. They were the heads of the family now.

Brenda sighed and said, "None of this should ever be shared with anyone else. I promised them that no one knew about what their mom did and I promised I would never talk about when she possessed me and spoke to them."

Carrie screamed and Angela said, "Mom. What are you saying? Possessed you, like a demon or a movie or something?"

Brenda did her best to explain but when she was saying it, she realized it sounded stupid and unbelievable. She could see from their faces that they thought it was not true. She tried to explain better, but it still did not sound right. Then she blurted out, "Just promise you can keep all of this secret. I mean it. Promise me."

Carrie spoke first and said, "I am never going to share that crazy story. Do not worry."

Angela said, "Me either. That is just a fantasy that she did that. Mom, just do not tell anyone else that. Seriously, they will think you are crazy."

Carrie laughed then and Angela joined in. Brenda felt herself starting to cry and was doing her best to hold it back. She felt very upset. They did not believe her and she had now double broken the promise. Suddenly she just hated Doris for making her part of her schemes. She started clearing the table and kept her back to the girls.

When they left, they hugged her and said, "Love you, Mom. Don't worry, your secret is safe with us!"

As she watched them pull out of the driveway in Angela's huge SUV, she did not believe them. They would tell their husbands. Maybe they would tell their friends. They were just like her and found it hard not to gossip. She thought she had done so well, but obviously, she was living her own sets of lies.

Simon

When Simon got back to Bellingham, he hit the ground running. He dove into work with more than his usual gusto. He painted his entire condo and redecorated his bedroom. He bought houseplants and a couple of new pictures for the walls. He bought a kayak and started kayaking on Sundays with a group of friends. He went to the brew pubs and he ate out with everyone he knew. He felt great.

Every Sunday evening, he and Laurel had a long phone conversation. They both had a glass of wine and talked about how things were going for them. He told her about the books he was working on at the job and all about his new kayak. He even told her he was trying to get

Mr. Pibbs outside on a leash. It was not going so great and most of the time he carried the chubby yellow kitty in his arms, but he wanted to at least try and get him some exercise.

Nate and Simon took up where they left off, working together and having drinks or going to movies. He told Nate about his Italian heritage and also about his mom's cancer and her choice to die with dignity, as they say. Nate was amazed at the secrets Simon's family could pull off. He shared that in his own big family, everyone knew everything and good luck hiding anything from them. He laughed and said, "That's why I am on the west coast. I just needed a little space."

Nate had started to see a woman he met through friends. Her name was Selene and she worked at the court house as a court clerk. He talked about her a lot and he seemed like he was falling deeply in love. Simon was so happy for him and asked if he could meet this wonder woman.

Nate and Selene invited him for dinner at Selene's tiny house that was in the backyard of her sister's house. Her sister had a huge home overlooking the water and she had offered her younger sister the rent of the "mother-in-law" unit that came with the house.

So, Simon put on a nice pair of jeans, his favorite sneakers and a button up shirt and headed over to meet Selene. He had been given instructions to drive down the alley and park in a spot next to the tiny house. He realized it was not as small as he imagined. It was painted to match the big house in front; pale green with cream colored trim. The front door was facing where he parked and it had a covered step into the house. Inside it was much lighter than he expected and it smelled like incense and lavender with something cooking in the kitchen as an undertone. Nate was seated on a comfortable couch holding a glass of whiskey. Selene greeted him at the door with a hug and he thought she was smelling him as they embraced.

She was beautiful. She was small and her hair was long and wavy and dark brown. She had an oval face with large brown eyes and deep dimples in her cheeks. She was dressed in some sort of caftan that was shades of blue. She had on dangling earrings with large blue and green sea glass beads on the ends of long silver chains. She was exotic looking and he felt like he wanted to stare at her and soak up whatever it was that she was about.

He did not realize that he was staring and he heard Nate say, "Okay Simon, come up for air! Selene is hot, no kidding and she is a great cook too."

Simon blushed and said, "Well, excuse me.

Your house is so lovely and it just feels great, I guess. I don't know what I am saying..."

Selene smiled and said, "What would you like to drink? I have vodka, whiskey, white or red wine and icy cold beer."

Simon gestured to Nate and said, "I'll have what he is having."

The evening got started. There were appetizers and drinks and quiet background music playing. Selene asked Simon a lot of questions and he found himself just answering them without any concern that she was too forward or nosey. He was mesmerized by her. Her voice had a slight trill to it and then it dropped a little into a smokey soft sound. She sat very still beside Nate with her hands in her lap. Nate had an amused look on his face and finally said, "Simon, I don't think Selene knows you are very private. I mean, you are talking more than I have ever heard you talk."

Selene patted Nate's leg and said, "Nate, you did not tell Simon the whole truth about me, did you? Simon, I am a psychic medium."

Simon looked at her and said, "No shit."

Selene laughed and said, "I can help you, if you have any questions about anything. I think you do. You have recently had an experience that opened you up to the other side. It's all around you. There is a certain vibration you are giving off."

Simon had not shared the "reveal" with Nate. He had told him the basics about his mom's death and the fact that he had recently found out he was not raised by his biological father. But Nate was the only person he had told and he kept the deeper parts to himself. After all, he had Laurel to talk to if he wanted.

Nate spoke up and said, "Hey, buddy, if you do not want to talk to Selene about anything that is fine. She just gets carried away sometimes. Selene, maybe he is not comfortable with that."

Selene ignored Nate and said, "Oh, he's comfortable. He was sent here. His mom wanted him to come. In fact, she has more information to share and he needs to hear it. Simon, after dinner, if you want, we can have a session."

Simon found himself saying, "That would be good." He could not believe he was saying that, but he was, so permission granted. While they ate the vegetarian meal she had prepared, he tried not to stare at her across the table. He was not attracted to her sexually. It was not like he was going to switch teams. It was just her way of talking and her confidence and caring. It was so comforting. Yes, comforting. He did not feel the least bit self-conscious. He just felt calm.

Nate was himself with her and it was nice to see him with someone he loved. Nate had not been happy in many relationships through the years. He kept picking the wrong women. He told Simon he thought he was trying to like the women he thought he should be with instead of just letting something happen. He had been raised to be ambitious and he thought he needed a partner who was just as ambitious as him. He did not want to have to explain his need to achieve and who could better understand that than a high achiever herself. But these relationships always turned out to be the wrong ones. Competitive and contentious were the best words to describe them. Nate would say "I am going to be single forever and I don't care." But Simon always thought Nate needed someone to love him and care for him. He had that kind of personality he had seen with some men. A woman who loves them and cares for them allows them to be what they need to be, which is masculine and focused. He looked at Selene and he knew he was looking at Nate's future.

After they finished dinner Selene lit candles, turned off the other lights and sat in an overstuffed chair, cross legged. Simon almost giggled out loud. It felt so typical of what he envisioned a medium would behave like. She instructed him to sit across from her on the couch and asked Nate to be completely quiet. And so, it began.

She talked quietly, her eyes were open, sometimes closing, and her body was still. She said, "Simon, your mother has something she needs you to understand. There was a man and she loved him. It was not something she did for excitement. She loved him. He was a beautiful soul. He walked away because there was no way he could support her and take her from her little daughter. He did not know about you, Simon, and she did not know herself until he had left. She wanted to tell him, but she loved him so much she did not want to be an anchor."

She paused, took a sip of water, and smoothed out her caftan. She looked at Simon closely and said, "There's more."

Simon nodded and thought, "I cannot wait to tell Laurel."

She continued. "You were a gift from him, her beautiful little Italian boy. You were the jewel in her crown. You were her favorite person in the world."

Then her tone changed a bit and she said, "Paul might have guessed, but if he did, he never spoke it out loud. She saw him look at you many times with suspicious eyes. He always felt separated from you two. That is why he focused so completely on Laurel. She was his connection to himself. She felt real to him."

Simon interrupted and said, "Can I ask questions?"

Selene shrugged and said, "Sometimes you can and sometimes you cannot."

Simon asked, "Why didn't you just tell me when I was old enough? It would have helped me."

Selene cocked her head to one side and said, "Just think about it. You will know the answer." Then she looked at Simon and said, "She has disconnected."

When Simon left Selene and Nate, he graciously thanked them for a wonderful evening. He hugged Selene extra hard and said, "What a deal, what a gift!" He said to Nate, "You have landed my friend."

As he was driving back to the condo, he played the conversation over and over in his mind. It would take a while to settle in. He felt happy and peaceful, but he had a small bit of skepticism lingering. He heard a voice in his head, not his mom, say "just let it be".

Laurel

It was almost November. The air was chilly and the garden was at rest. What a whirl-wind September and October had been. She had too much produce, so she consulted with Uncle Mike and he suggested she take some to the Farmer's Market in Yakima and try to sell some to fruit stands. He also helped her find a group of high school kids who would pick the apples for her. She worked beside them of course; they stayed focused that way.

She sold all of the apples which was amaz-ing to her. She took boxes of tomatoes, pep-pers, corn, onions and eggs to the Farmer's Market. She sold potatoes and apples to the fruit stands. She put together bouquets of zinnias, asters, dahlias, sunflowers, and baby's breath and sold them at the Farmer's Market too. She actually painted a sign and named her stall, Olsen Farm. She painted an apple tree and a fence on the sign. Her painting was better than she thought it would be and she thought that would be a logo she could design, just in case she wanted to keep growing and selling.

She froze vegetables and invested in a new freezer. It was a big upright and she fixed up a room in the shed for it. She built potato and onion bins in the same room and hung garlic and hot peppers from the ceiling. She also put her canning on the shelves beside it and called the room her produce room. She painted another sign for the door.

She went to see Uncle Peter every other day. He finally accepted that she was his contact to the outside world. She made her way into the old house to see what kind of supplies he needed on a weekly basis.

She would never forget the first foray into that place. She pulled up to the house and all was as she remembered, if not worse. The house was just visible through old vining roses and ivy and weeds taller than her. She could see an old apple tree with dried-up apples on it and several lilac trees that she knew her Grandma Gerda had treasured. The porch was dilapidated and there was no way to enter the front door. The path to the back door was narrow and it had stones that had been laid at some point to delineate the route. It was over-grown with dry weeds and she brushed them back as she made her way to the backdoor.

The backdoor was surrounded by an en-closed porch with old rusted screens that no longer served their function. The floor was splintered and the backdoor itself was actu-ally the most intact things she had encoun-tered. She knocked and there was no answer. She turned the knob and stepped into the world of Peter.

The kitchen was the first room. It still had all the things in it she remembered from Grand-ma Gerda. It was large and the wall paper was peeling. It had once been apple trees in a striped pattern. It was now yellowed and dirty with grease and smoke. There was still a wood cooking stove in one corner and an electric one that must have been at least from the 1950s on the opposite side of the kitchen. A small table had replaced the large one that now sat in Laurel's kitchen and it was really just a card table. One chair was sitting there and it was an old wooden one with cracking paint. There were no curtains left on the win-dows, just some shreds of fabric hanging off of the curtain rods. There was dust thick on everything and it smelled dirty and greasy.

She called out for Peter, but no answer. So, she opened the old fridge and looked inside. She saw a block of cheese, a jar of milk, brown eggs, and a few tomatoes. There was a box of Pepsi cans that was half full. The freezer had nothing in it.

She looked at the counters and found one loaf of bread, white, half eaten, and a few apples in a bowl. She also found a box of wheat cereal and a bowl of sugar. This was enough to make a weekly shopping list.

She wished she knew what he liked that her mom made. She remembered biscuits and cake were things that were taken over there a lot. So, she could make a cake and a batch of biscuits every week, no problem.

She called for Peter again. She heard some shuffling in the next room, so she opened the door into the living room or whatever it might have once been, maybe a dining room opening into a small living room. Either way, now it was just old newspapers, empty cardboard boxes, dust inches thick, spider webs and the smell of something decaying. The windows were filthy and only let through a murky light. She did not see Peter.

So, she said out loud, "Okay Uncle Peter. This is Laurel, Paul's daughter. I am going to do your shopping for you and you will need to talk to me if you want something more than I bring. You can talk to me. I am the one who will be taking care of you now."

Still no response, so she went back out the back door and headed to the pickup. When she backed out and turned to leave, she thought she saw him looking out one of the dirty living room windows, but it could have been a ghost. Peter was a living ghost for sure.

Her routine with Peter was every two days, she pulled in, checked the food supplies, left some kind of sweet treat, and talked to him like he was in the room. She talked about the weather and the harvest. She told him about selling fruits and vegetables at the market. Sometimes she washed up the dishes in the sink and she slowly started a routine of small cleaning projects. She did not want to freak him out with too much tidying up all at once, but she managed to clear spaces slowly. One day she got up on the counter and took down the fabric shreds from the curtain rods. She set some mouse traps under the sink and in the corners and most days she hauled out a couple of dead mice. Then she put poison under the sink too and slowly started to cut back the mouse population.

She bought a clear plastic bread loaf container and put the bread in it. She knew he would eat the bread even if a mouse had helped themselves. She put a butter dish that was clear on the counter too. All this took place over days and it seemed that Peter was accepting it because anything she did was not undone the next time she came.

Then one day near the beginning of October, he was standing in the kitchen when she came in. He was his usual filthy self. He did not make eye contact but said, "Little Laurel".

Laurel answered, "Yes. It is me."

Each day she came after that he came into the kitchen and either sat there or stood there while she tidied up and put things in the fridge. He accepted the new pants and shirts she brought and socks and underwear. She handed him a laundry basket and said, "Every day, take off all your clothes and put them in this basket. I will wash them for you."

Then she brought in a little plastic cleaning tote with shampoo, bar soap, toothbrush and toothpaste and a comb in it. She put it on the kitchen counter and said, "Use these things to wash yourself Peter. You really smell terrible."

He did do a kind of washing of his body and it looked like he was doing it at the kitchen sink and he was changing his clothes. They were now connected and Laurel knew she would be the one to make sure that when he needed it, he would be taken care of until the end. Right now, he was someone that she loved and she had never really realized that before. It felt good to take care of him.

Mike checked in too, but he could see that Laurel was making progress. Sometimes he would call her and make a suggestion and one day when she came, she saw his truck there and it was filled with some of the cardboard boxes and newspapers from the living room. He was part of the cleanup crew now. Uncle Mike was a good man.

Life for Laurel was full of everyday tasks that she was finding great pleasure in doing. She had many ideas for improvements to her house, as she was beginning to think of it as hers. She was planning to clean out the barn and had a thought about making it into a produce stand of her own. She was busy planning and felt better than she had felt in years. Life on the Olsen Farm was what she needed. She felt free.

She thought about taking a job of some sort. She was so geared to the outdoors she thought maybe farm work would be the best bet. She knew she could do most things that a farm hand would do, even though now she would probably need to speak Mexican in order to work on a farm. But that would be good. She could speak passable Spanish and she could adapt.

She started visiting some of the truck farms in the area to see what they might need as far as help. She got to know people that way.

Some were people she had known all her life and some of them were new to the Yakima Valley. A lot of the farms that she remembered had now been bought up by big corporate operations. Things had changed a lot, but it still was one of the best places in the entire state to grow produce. She had finally come to realize that was her calling; growing food.

One of the places she visited was Maria's husbands' operation. It was called Mountain View Farm. It was impressive. She called Maria first and told her she would like to tour the farm and set up a time to meet with her and her husband, Jake. She knew Jake from high school. He really did not look at all like she remembered. He used to be tall and wide with curly black hair. He was still tall and wide, but his hair was salt and pepper gray and he a strangely large moustache. This was something she kept seeing all around the valley. It was not in style anywhere else.

Jake was a nice man and Maria was just plain annoying. She also did not know anything about the operations and she just wanted to gossip about how things were going with their friend Carla. Laurel did not want to be too rude to her, but luckily Jake spoke up and said, "Maria, could you go and get us some cold drinks?"

When she flitted away, Jake said, "She is still

the same as high school." He smiled broadly and chuckled.

Jake gave her some good ideas about starting a small operation of her own. She also asked if he had any need for some help and he said he was pretty well set up with the Garcia family that worked for him and some of their relatives from Texas. But he did know of someone who was looking for some help and that was a guy named Brad Collier. He told her where he lived and even called Brad while she was there and made an introduction.

By the time she left she felt good about the visit and she thought Jake was a good man. He even seemed to think Maria was amusing and not just plain annoying. Laurel thought, love is strange.

Brad Collier's place was smaller than Jake's Mountain View Farm. It consisted of an old two-story farm house, several sheds and a barn. He had row crops and some grapes and a small orchard of peaches on one side of the driveway and nectarines on the other side. When she pulled in a big collie came out to greet her barking and wagging its tail. She heard a deep voice say, "Peaches, settle down."

Out strode Brad Collier. He was a nice surprise. He was tall and slim and he had on a baseball cap with some curly brown hair coming out of it. He was tanned and rugged, but his eyes were sparkly and his smile was huge. He did not have the big mustache either; a bonus. He shook her hand and said, "You must be Laurel. Jake called. Nice to meet ya." His hand was rough but big and warm.

She stuttered and said, "Yes, thank you for meeting with me. Nice to meet you too."

Brad asked her to come inside for a cup of coffee and when she went in the house she could tell he was not married. It was a man's house. No touch of a woman. It was tidy, but sparce and the coffee was strong and black.

They spent several hours talking about truck gardening, prices, weather, sales, building a clientele, finding help, etc. The conversation flowed easily and it was obvious that they both knew a lot about growing food, but less about making money that way. They were talking so much that Laurel forgot she was inquiring about work, so she asked, "Brad, do you have any part time work I could do for you?"

Brad said he could use a few hours of help with some fall clean up and some other things. He said, "I mean, I don't have enough money for a full time hired hand, but it sounds like you are busy with your own place."

Laurel looked at him and said, "Maybe we can swap. I'll do some things for you and you do some things for me. We could figure out how many hours a week we could each give and just call it even. If it doesn't work out, then we can fire each other."

Brad chuckled and stuck out his big weathered farm hand and said, "It's a deal. Let's give it a shot."

Laurel pulled out of the driveway in her '68 Ford pickup and smiled a huge smile. It was not just her, but there was a spark there and it felt good. Was this the beginning of something, or was it the end of one thing and the beginning of another? Or was it fate or was it accidental? As Laurel drove home from her visit with Brad Collier she felt something she had not felt in ages. She was attracted to him sexually and intellectually and she wanted to know more about him. And so, the relationship began.

Brenda

It was the week of Thanksgiving. It had always been a holiday she looked forward to. There was not the pressure of Christmas. They had celebrated many happy ones. This year her daughter Angela had suggested that they gather at her house. Brenda knew it was for a very kind reason. They thought she was aging out of holding the big dinners and her daughters wanted to lighten her load. What a kind thing, but it left Brenda feeling a little useless.

She had suggested she could still make the pies and Angela said, "Okay, but your oldest granddaughter is planning to make an apple pie and Carrie wants to make the pumpkin. Maybe you could bring some kind of yummy bars."

Brenda wanted to scream, "Bars! Yummy bars! They are not a Thanksgiving tradition! Why do I have to make something no one is looking forward to?"

She thought back to last year's celebration. Paul and Doris had been there with Laurel. Simon had celebrated with friends in Bellingham. Had the pies not been up to snuff? Was her turkey dry? She did not think so, but she was a little worried.

She decided against making some kind of "bar". To hell with that. Instead, she would make a layer cake, chocolate, and decorate it with fall leaves. It would be very beautiful and she would put it on her mother's gorgeous crystal cake stand. They were not fully in charge of her yet.

She called Laurel and asked if she and Simon were planning a celebration or would they like to be included with her family. Laurel said Simon was coming but they would have dinner together and come over for pie, if that was okay. Brenda thought to herself, "No one comes over for cake on Thanksgiving or for bars."

Brenda had been talking to Laurel on the phone off and on, but she did not go to see her often. Laurel was busy and she was establishing herself as a permanent resident. Her own place and now her work with Brad Collier were taking up most of her time. Brenda was so happy for Laurel. She had found what she really wanted to do. How very lucky for her and how brave that she walked away from the city life. Brenda really did not want to interfere in any way.

Brenda found she had too much spare time, so she decided to continue the story she had started about her sister and the illness. She fictionalized it enough, but some of it was an exact mirror of Doris and her life. She was spending time each day, writing a little, re-writing, and generally doubting that anyone would want to ever read it. But even if it sat in a bottom drawer in her desk and was never read, she was enjoying writing it.

There was only one part of Doris' life that she had never shared with Laurel and Simon and that was Doris' time in the psych ward at the hospital in Yakima. It had happened three times and it was horrible for the adults, but Doris asked her to never mention it to the children. They were little ones and were not in school yet when it first happened. They were told that their mom was in Seattle visiting one of her dear friends. The children were able to stay with Brenda and Mike and had built in playmates with Angela and Carrie. Brenda cared for all four of the little ones while try-ing to find a way to visit her sister. Mostly she watched them play and worried herself sick.

During this time, she thought about the fact that Doris could be permanently crazy and if she was, what if Mike and Brenda had to take on the two children? They had room and the children were not bad children, quite the opposite. It would be doable, but what about Paul? What if he demanded they stay with him and then he could not really do all they needed and then Brenda thought, I would just be going over there constantly trying to cover what he was missing. That sounded horrible.

Really, she did not want to have four children. She had always thought two was enough and the thought of four all of the time was overwhelming. Plus, would she just favor Angela and Carrie so much that everyone would grow up resenting her? That was such a real possibility. Or the opposite, she could over protect Doris' children and her own girls would always hold it against her. She was a young woman but she was fully aware of the pitfalls of raising children. So many things go wrong no matter how hard you try.

The hospitalizations took place over two years. The diagnosis at that time was "nervous breakdown". Doris was 27 years old. It was two years after Simon was born and it happened in the summer, then the following winter and once more in the next summer. By the third one, Paul knew the signs and was quick to call Brenda and let her know he had to take Doris back to the 5th floor, as it was referred to locally. That was the psych ward.

The first time it happened Brenda was picking peas in her garden and the girls were playing with their dolls in the yard. It was unusually hot and Brenda was about ready to stop for the afternoon when she heard a pick-up skid into her driveway. She could not see the driveway from the garden, but suddenly there was Paul standing with Simon on his hip and holding Laurel's hand. He looked terrified and said, "Please watch the kids for me Brenda. It's Doris. I've got to take her to a hospital."

"Oh my God. What happened Paul?"

"I don't know, she just is crying and babbling and won't eat and she won't bath and I think she has to go to the hospital." Paul burst into tears.

Brenda called to her girls who were 9 and 7 to come and take the children. She said, "Now why don't you all go play by the garden, run along now."

She grabbed Paul's arm and walked with him to the other side of the house. He was shaking. "How long has she been doing this? I talked to her two days ago and she sounded tired, but she didn't tell me she was upset."

Paul shook his head and said, "I have to get back there Brenda. I am so worried. I think she might kill herself."

Brenda said, "Go, just go. Call me as soon as you can. Oh my God, Paul."

Brenda remembered standing there shaking and crying and trying to pull herself together for the children. She needed to be home with the children but she really needed to be there for Doris too. After all, Paul did not know about Diego and Brenda really thought that this was the root of what was happening. Doris never talked about Diego, but she looked sad and was much quieter these days.

When Mike got home, Brenda told him what happened and that she was waiting to hear from Paul. He said, "Go. I can handle the little ones. I'll call my sister Janis and she can come help me. Just go, Brenda."

It was a whirlwind after that. Doris was admitted to the psych ward very quickly. Brenda and Paul were not allowed to see her and were told that she would be sedated and examined by the psychologist and by a medical doctor.

They sat together in the waiting room. Brenda had tried to get Paul to talk about what had been going on, but he seemed to be in a state of shock and was not giving more than one-word answers. When a doctor came to get them, they were told she would be staying overnight and possibly for several days. They said she had a nervous breakdown and with time and medication they thought she could resume her normal life. They asked, "Has there been a particular trauma that she has experienced?"

Brenda could not say anything. Paul said, "No. She has a 2-year-old and a 5-year-old and she has been doing great."

Brenda nodded and her stomach knotted up. She wanted to tell the doctor, but how could she? Would Doris say something during the counseling or whatever they were going to do with her? Were they just going to give her so much dope she would just clam up? She started crying and she felt like she cried inwardly for days after that.

So, this day before Thanksgiving as she put the final touches on her beautiful cake, she found herself wondering if this was something she needed to share with Laurel and Simon. Paul had never told them. He was so ashamed that it even happened. There was no chance he could ever talk about it. It was better to keep that secret buried, she decided. Enough trauma and adjustments for Laurel and Simon had already taken place.

Simon

It was good to be going home for Thanksgiving. Home to his sister and the renewed life of the Olsen Farm. He brought frozen blueberries from the Whatcom County fields and he planned to make a beautiful pie. He knew Laurel had so much homegrown food, but he wanted to contribute. Several bottles of good wine, some craft beer and a baggie full of joints. He planned to stay until Sunday.

When he got there, he saw his sister was driving the tractor into the shed and he thought she looked right at home. When she saw him, she leapt down from the tractor seat and ran across the driveway. "Hey my baby brother! I am so glad you are here!"

They hugged and then she helped him bring in his bag and box of goodies. Everything looked familiar to him, but it smelled different in the house and it felt light. He wondered about Selene the medium and if she could feel what he was feeling; a house at peace.

It was Wednesday afternoon and Simon jumped in and helped Laurel with the things she was preparing. He popped open a nice bottle of wine, poured their glasses full and then he said, "A toast, to my marvelous sister in her beautiful home."

Laurel smiled and said, "I haven't felt like this, ever, Simon. I didn't even know how unhappy I was before." She sighed and went back to cutting up the bread to toast for the dressing.

They talked a lot that day. Laurel kept bringing up Brad and Simon teased her about finally meeting her mate. Laurel cautioned, "We just work together now. I mean, maybe there will be more, I mean, I hope there will be. I'm just a little nervous about it. Been so long and I guess I have never given my heart to anyone."

Simon looked at her and said, "I hear ya sis. I don't know why it is so hard for you and me, but it sounds like he is a good person and you guys like all of the same things."

Laurel told him that Brad was spending Thanksgiving with his family in Oregon or she would have had them meet each other. "He knows all about you, Simon. He is probably nervous to meet the brother 'who walks on water'!"

They talked about Selene the medium and how they both just believed in being able to reach the deceased now. The "reveal" had been one thing, now with the additional information from the medium, they were converts. Not that they were going to start reading Tarot cards and visit psychics. They just felt like it was another part of life and you don't need all the answers to believe it.

Then the subject of the Thanksgiving dinner at Angela's came up. Simon said he was glad that they were only going for dessert. "You know, Angela and Carrie are kind of snobs. They always make me feel like the only reason they are nice to me is because of their mom."

Laurel laughed and told him, "Seriously, I never go see them, Simon. We are just so different and they can make some pretty snide remarks. I just decided it doesn't matter if I am related and they live like 3 miles away, I am too busy to waste my time trying to understand them."

"So, I guess this pie thing tomorrow is just a courtesy visit, for Aunt Brenda and Uncle Mike, right? I mean we can eat and run. Maybe the chickens will need to be fed!"

Laurel smiled and laughed and took a big gulp of the delicious wine and said, "Let's get stoned!"

The next morning, they got up and had coffee

sitting in the newly decorated living room. Laurel had painted it a color called soft clay, which was basically beige. The curtains were a light green color and were old fashioned with tie backs. The couch was small and was a beautiful green and light maroon floral print. There were two new overstuffed rockers that were a coordinating green with a maroon stripe. The new rug was beige and tan with a swirling pattern. Everything was modern and old fashioned at the same time. Simon praised Laurel's decorating ability and saw that she had incorporated some of her parent's pictures and her mom's glass vases were on the mantel, much like their mom had displayed them.

The day was before them and they felt good. Laurel took Simon with her over to Uncle Peter's house and she told him he had to come inside even though he was reluctant. Peter was standing in the kitchen with clean clothes on and his wild hair a bit combed. He said, "Diego is here."

They put him between them in the pick-up and took him to Laurel's house for the feast. He was his usual quiet self. Simon said to Laurel, "I am glad you have taken him under your wing, sis. He deserves it."

Laurel said, "Oh, and Uncle Mike is a big part of it too. Like I told you, he has hauled off loads of junk and repaired small things. We are going slow for Peter's sake."

Dinner was delicious, working together and laughing about how their dad always had to eat a turkey sandwich with his dinner. They talked about making their mom's dressing the same way she did and Laurel told Simon, no, we are not adding chestnuts. Maybe next year.

Around 5:00 they returned Peter to his house. You could tell when he wanted to go because he would stand at the back door and stare out. That was the signal.

About 6:00 Brenda called and said that it was going to be time for dessert soon so come on over. Before they left, they tried to figure out something they could take for Angela, the hostess. Laurel had been putting things in her parent's old bedroom that she was not going to keep, but wanted Simon to go through them before she took them to Good Will. He suggested maybe there was something of their mom's they could give Angela.

They found just the right thing, they thought. It was a tea pot that had beautiful orange and yellow chrysanthemums painted on it. It was in perfect shape as their mom always kept it in the glass cupboard in the dining room. Simon did not want it and they both thought it was a nice gift.

They drove over to Angela's, a little drunk, but not noticeably so. Laurel drove the truck and Simon cradled the tea pot. They did not anticipate what would happen next.

Angela & Carrie

Angela had worked hard and so had Carrie to make this a beautiful day. The table had been decorated with the utmost care, looking at web sites for the perfect center pieces for the holiday table in the formal dining area. Angela had set it up so that 8 people could sit around the main table (the adults and the 2 oldest grandchildren) and had set up a smaller table in the same room for the other 4 children. She used her paternal grandmother's good China dishes and she bought new matching water and wine glasses to match.

There were name placards and candles during dinner and a nice local white wine was served with the turkey. Everyone said the dinner was delicious. Angela beamed and Carrie said, "Yes, thank you for hosting us Ang. It's just beautiful."

Angela said, "Well, Carrie, I could not have done it without you."

The dinner had been put away, the coffee was now on and Angela arranged the pies and her mother's cake on the main table. More candles were lit and her new turkey dessert plates were placed on the table too. She and Carrie had been throwing each other secret (they thought) glances all day about their mother's cake. Carrie whispered to Angela as they were cutting the raw vegetables for a tray, "It is so gaudy. I mean, those gum paste leaves must have come from the dollar store."

Angela giggled and said, "They did. She told me."

The grandchildren were excited over the cake but Brenda had noticed that her daughters were laughing about it while the children were all taking secret little licks of the frosting on their fingers. She was not feeling so great today about the way her daughters were behaving. She would have used the word snob herself if she had been telling someone about them.

When Laurel and Simon arrived, Brenda lit up. Angela and Carrie noticed it and Carrie said, "Here we go. The favorites are here." She said it under her breath, but did not realize that Angela's youngest daughter had heard her. She was only 4 and she said, "I am Grandma's favorite, not these guys."

Everyone tried to ignore the comment and Angela whispered to her daughter, "Yes you are darling."

Simon set the teapot on the kitchen counter and explained that it was their mom's and they thought maybe Angela would like to have it. Angela graciously said, "Thank you so much. How beautiful and from Aunt Doris. I appreciate that very much."

Carrie picked it up and said, "This was always in that glass cabinet, up on the top. I remember it."

Laurel had a feeling that they should have brought something for Carrie too, so she said, "Carrie, I have some other things of my mom's you could choose from if you would like to. There are some old vases and things that are quite pretty."

Carrie chuckled and said, "Oh, no thank you. I am a very modern girl. I think it's better in your farm house."

Simon tipped his head and could not suppress a grin. Laurel just acted like she did not hear her. Then Simon spotted the chocolate layer cake and said, "Oh my gosh. Is that your chocolate layer cake Auntie?"

Brenda beamed and said, "Yes, it is honey! I did not get to make pies this year, so I just decided to start a new tradition, Thanksgiving cake."

Angela and Carrie rolled their eyes at each other, which Laurel caught and so she chimed in with Simon. "I love that idea. I think I will start doing that too."

Soon the pies and the cake were being cut and the men were taking theirs into the living room for the football game (minus Simon) and the children were outside and upstairs playing. Simon, Laurel, Angela, Carrie and Brenda were sitting at the main table. Conversation was polite and low key. Things were going as well as can be expected when Angela said, "Well, Laurel, I am happy you decided to stay in your parent's house, but I was surprised you did not want to return to Seattle."

Laurel said, "I guess my heart is in farming Angela. I am really grateful that I can do what I love now."

Carrie said, "Yes, and just being given a farm, I mean that is some good luck. I mean, you could use some good luck what with all the things that have been thrown at you this year. Your mom taking her own life, your dad's sudden death and then the DNA. You needed some good luck."

Laurel and Simon looked at each other and then at Brenda. Simon spoke first. "I was not aware that you knew about mom or that you knew about the DNA test. Aunt Brenda said she kept it between her and Uncle Mike."

"Oh Simon," said Angela, "you must know by now that mom cannot keep a secret. I could not believe she did not tell you about your real dad a long time ago. It was ridiculous."

"Excuse me. It was not ridiculous. My sister asked me not to, so that's why I did it." Brenda's lip was quivering.

"Jeez Mom, I think you took that a little too far, don't you? I mean, Aunt Doris had a lot of drama in her life. Remember the stays in the psych ward", said Angela.

Laurel said, "My goodness Angela. You are just full of information. It seems you might know more about my life than I did. And Aunt Brenda, seriously, you told them, but we had to wait? That is a bit bizarre."

Carrie piped in, "It is! I was 7 when she was admitted to the 5th floor and we heard Mom and Dad talking about it. But she told us to stop asking questions and go play with Laurel. So, you know, we thought someone told you later."

Simon sat very still and he said to Laurel, "Did you know? I mean, you didn't know she was on the 5th floor, right?"

Laurel looked at him angrily and said, "Hell no Simon! If I did, I would have told you. Brenda, why didn't you tell us this when you told us all about Diego?"

Brenda was sniffling now and she said, "Because, I thought you had too much trauma already. Then Doris decides to tell you about her suicide..."

Simon snapped, "Hey it was not exactly a suicide. She took herself out to keep all of us from suffering too."

Angela said, "Well, it was kind of a suicide. I mean she was on suicide watch for several years after she went in the loony bin. She finally just had a reason to do it, I think."

Laurel said, "Wow, Angela, you can really be a bitch sometimes, but seriously, you are overstepping right now."

Carrie jumped in and said, "Well, it is just the truth Laurel. My mom has protected you from the truth our whole lives. I guess we were not supposed to be upset by the truth but yes, we must protect little Laurel and weird Simon. Jesus."

Suddenly Uncle Mike was standing there and he was looming over the table. "That is enough. That is absolutely the last I want to hear of any of this. Shut it down now."

He took Brenda by the arm and walked her out the back door and they all heard their car drive away. Simon and Laurel stood up at the same time and without saying a word, walked out and climbed into the pick-up.

That would be a Thanksgiving they would never forget.

Laurel/Simon

The evening was spent talking, of course. There was so much to process and it would take longer than one evening, but they tried to get their heads around it.

They were both a little bit surprised at how resentful their cousins were toward them and Aunt Brenda. They always knew they were all different but they never knew to what extent it had affected Angela and Carrie. They were both angry and they blamed Doris and Brenda. Obviously, they were not fond of Laurel and Simon, but was it mostly based in the resentment they felt about the secret keeping and how it affected them?

Simon wondered why they never told them

anything before now. He said, what about the sleep overs and the summer picnics? There would have been many times they could have slipped up or purposely told them, since they were so resentful.

Laurel had some compassion for them. She thought that Doris' trauma had taken part of their mother away from them. She even said that if she had kids, they might resent her relationship with Simon. She was trying to understand it.

Simon on the other hand just thought they were bitches and that was his final statement on that part of the story. He thought they were small minded and judgmental of anyone who did not do what they found acceptable. Laurel understood that because he was after all, the most "different" in his sexual orientation and his heritage, but she too thought they were completely out of line and used the word "mean" more than once.

The talk about their mom was the biggest hurdle for them both. How had they lived without ever realizing how fragile their mom was? Simon felt like he had been so messed up as a kid that he could not see it because he was struggling to make it through his own situation. Laurel said she got that, but that he had been a sensitive person too. So, how did they both miss it?

They tried to recall things that happened that might have been clues. Laurel remembered one Christmas when their dad put up the tree and wrapped the gifts. They thought it was funny and that their mom was just trying to make him participate. But then they thought about Christmas morning and the lack of cinnamon rolls and their mom came down late for the Santa Claus surprises. Simon remembered she stayed in a robe that day and they went to Aunt Brenda's for dinner. Laurel remembered their mom was "sick" and stayed home. Now they thought it must have been an episode or something. They thought they were about 7 and 10 years old at the time.

Simon thought they should go through old letters and paperwork the next day to see if they could find any more clues to their childhood. Laurel agreed and when they finally went to bed it was past 2 a.m. Even then, they both laid in their beds and tried to envision their childhood in a new light. It was not very easy to do.

The next day was an unusually warm November day. All the leaves had fallen already, but the air still had the smell of fall. Laurel went out and fed the chickens and left the barn kitties some turkey scraps. She went to the produce room in the shed and brought in a jar of canned peaches to go with breakfast. Simon was cooking and he had requested some peaches to go with his crepes. It was a nice morning except for the lingering strangeness of the day before.

When Laurel sat down for her coffee she said, "Simon, do you think we will hear from Aunt Brenda any time soon?"

Simon did not answer right away and when he did, he sounded a little angry. "I do not know. I feel like I do not know anything about this family right now, except that you are my sister and I can trust you. The rest of our family is untrustworthy. Except for Uncle Peter. Thank God he is incapable of lying. 'Diego is here!'"

Laurel smiled when he mentioned Uncle Peter. Yes, he was a simple man and he was easy to understand, even with his eccentric ways. He was just Peter and he never tried to be anyone else. That was the nicest thing about it. No pretenses needed.

Laurel said, "Well, I think she will steer clear for a while, but she will want to reconnect pretty quickly. She is not a loner and her daughters have really been hard on her. She will need some love. She will come and see me I think."

Simon agreed, "Oh yeah, she will and so will Uncle Mike. He was ashamed of his daughters yesterday. It was so plainly stated by the look on his face. All of that drama would not have happened if Angela and Carrie would have just shut up."

Laurel chuckled and said, "Yep. It would have just been another uncomfortable dessert around the Thanksgiving table. Starring the 'Mean Sisters' and the 'Weird Cousins'!"

They ate the crepes which were delicious. They cleaned up the kitchen and then they headed upstairs to the attic. Laurel had not tackled it yet. It was a typical creepy space, spiders included and dust on everything. Most of the contents were childhood things of theirs and some old Christmas decorations. Laurel had wanted to go through them to see if Simon wanted to take anything with him, so they hauled down those Christmas boxes.

Next, they looked for pictures, paperwork, or anything else they thought might help them to better understand what circumstances they grew up in. They found about three boxes that fit that description and brought them down too.

They put all the boxes in the living room. They dusted them and even opened the front door and a window to let out the dust in the air. They settled into the new chairs and each took a box and started the search.

At first it was tax returns and farming receipts. Laurel made an area that she called "burn pile" and they planned a nice fall afternoon fire in the fire pit out back. There were a few insurance papers about the house that she wanted to hold onto. She already had copies of the titles to everything in a small safe she had purchased.

Of course, her parents never had health insurance so there was not a lot of information about medical bills. In fact, there were none. Laurel looked at Simon and said, "How in the hell did they pay for her hospitalizations? They were not free. I hadn't thought about that. Dad was so cheap, I just can't imagine how freaked out he would have been if he got a big bill from the hospital."

Simon stopped going through his box and said, "I have no idea. I mean, you are right it would have been a huge deal to him. How could he keep from just blowing his stack every time she had to go back?"

They found nothing about any hospital expenses or even information about their mom's cancer appointments. Simon sighed and said, "I know mom's diagnosis was bad, but you know, she probably felt guilty for all that she had already cost dad in their marriage, and cancer would not have been cheap with no insurance. Neither of them was old enough for Medicare. God, they were ridiculous, Laurel."

Laurel said, "I know. It's hard to understand them. I am lost right now."

So, they tackled the Christmas decorations. There were some good memories in those boxes, but all tainted with the problem of not knowing what had been going on while they thought it was all okay, if not perfect.

Simon found an antique Santa from Norway that had been Grandma Gerda's. It did not look like an American Santa. It was a gnome figure with a long white beard and a red hat. It was about 10 inches tall and Grandma had brought it with her when she immigrated. Laurel kept her mother's Christmas candy dishes and her Christmas table clothes and runners. Many of the things had not been used for a long time, so they made a box for Good Will.

This took until late afternoon. They cleaned up the mess and headed into the kitchen for a Thanksgiving meal repeat. They made a box of goodies for Uncle Peter and Simon said he would take them over before they ate.

When he pulled into Uncle Peter's house to his surprise, Peter was standing at the back door waiting. He smiled and said, "Diego is here." Simon smiled back and said, "Diego has some goodies for you Uncle Peter."

Simon put the things in the refrigerator that would spoil. He looked around the kitchen and he could tell that Uncle Mike and Laurel had been doing a lot of things to improve the house. He noticed a new faucet had been installed and some curtains were hanging. There was a table cloth on the little table and another chair had been added. He noticed the new rag rug in front of the sink and the new dish towel hanging.

Uncle Peter was helping himself to a piece of blueberry pie. Simon looked at him and he was filled with love. Peter knew who Simon was and he did not care. He decided he wanted to do something for Peter that was just from him. He knew what that would be and when he left, he said, "I will be back tomorrow, Uncle Peter."

Peter said, "Diego is here."

The next day Simon returned with the Norwegian Gnome and a new coat that he had just bought for himself. It had a down lining in bright green and the outer fabric was a waxed canvas fabric in a beautiful rich brown. Simon loved that coat, but he thought Uncle Peter needed it more than him. He made Peter put it on and he asked if he could take away the old dirty one on the peg by the back door.

Uncle Peter stroked the bright green lining and he said, "I like my new coat, Diego." So, Simon took the old one and put the Norwegian Gnome in the kitchen window. No one besides Laurel felt more like family that day. Simon smiled to himself as he drove away and thought, he's not even really my uncle.

Brenda

The day after Thanksgiving had always been the day that Brenda got out her Christmas decorations and put them up. She knew just where they were and she usually asked Mike to help her bring the boxes into the living room so she could start decorating. But on this day after the total blow up at Angela's, she did not feel like doing it.

Mike asked her if she wanted help and she said, no, but she did not say, I am not going to put anything up this year. That was what she was thinking. She felt deflated. She realized how angry her own children were at her and she had been skimming over that for so long. There were always some snide comments and they always gossiped about Laurel and Simon, but she felt that they actually hated them now.

She was thinking about her own relationship with her niece and nephew. She had always been trying to fill up the holes here and there that were created by Doris and Paul too. But she always thought she had done a good job with her own girls at the same time. Obviously, they did not think so.

She wondered if they would ever understand why she did the things that she did for her sister. She knew her daughters were close to each other, but their lives had been easy so far. No traumas that were life changing. Neither of them had experienced the death of a parent or a child or of a lost romance. Both of them married their first loves and as far as she knew they were still in love with their husbands. Part of her resented their perfect little lives made possible by her and Mike. But that was not completely true either. They had made things work themselves. Brenda and Mike had just eased them along.

Mike had been very quiet on the way home. In fact, he was quiet when they got home and that morning too. He looked concerned, but he was not the type to talk about it. Whatever he was thinking was pretty straight forward. She knew he was disgusted by the conversation at Angela's and she knew he would always support his wife. She doubted he would say anything to his daughters. Leaving abruptly had said it all. The girls would know how angry he was without him saying a word.

Brenda wanted to talk to Laurel and Simon. She wanted to tell them that their mother had fought hard to stay well. She wanted to tell them that when Doris was just 13 years old, she had run away with one of the neighbor boys. It was summer time, hot and dry. The neighbor's name was Danny Gordon and she knew the two of them had kissed each other when they were out riding horses. She also knew that her sister wrote poems about him at night and she wandered off when they were doing chores to meet him.

For some reason the two of them decided they would run away and camp on the Yakima River. It was pretty polluted back then from all the fertilizer run off from the crops, but kids would swim it anyway. So, they both snuck a change of clothes, some food and towels and one early morning about 4:00 they met up in the field behind the house and crossed fences and pastures and fields to the river.

Brenda had slept through it all and when she woke up the next morning, she looked over at her sister's bed and thought, wow, Doris got up before me. Doris had always been the one who wanted to sleep in and took about an hour to fully wake up. Brenda was a person whose feet hit the floor and she was wide awake. She went down to the kitchen and her mother was washing fresh cherries in the sink. She said her usual sweet "Good morning honey", and brought Brenda a fresh stack of pancakes.

Brenda said, through a mouthful of syrup and pancake, "Where's Doris? I can't believe she got up before me."

Her mother turned and said, "She is up? Why didn't she come in for breakfast? That girl. Do you think she is already on that horse? She lives on that horse these days..."

Brenda finished the pancakes and went outside to see if Doris' horse, Windy, was in her stall or in the pasture. Before she got into the barn, she saw Windy running in the pasture. She thought maybe Doris had let her into the pasture so she walked through the barn hollering her name. No answer.

Brenda's dad was out in one of the orchards picking up the boxes of cherries as the pickers finished them with his tractor and trailer. She could hear the tractor, but she knew Doris hated picking cherries, so she probably was not there.

She went back to the house and said, "Mom, the horse is here but I can't find Brenda."

Her mother looked worried and said, "Well, that is unusual. You are sure she wasn't in the bathroom or something?"

Brenda said, "Nope."

Then her mother said, "Maybe she is with Danny. I swear she has a bad crush on that kid."

Her mother took the phone off the hook and dialed Danny's house. His mother answered and Brenda listened to her mother say, "Hi there Carol. Hey, I am sorry to call so early, but have you seen Doris this morning? I thought maybe she and Danny were out in the field or something."

Whatever Danny's mother said upset Brenda's mother because she said abruptly, "Well, I am sorry you feel that way Carol. Can you please ask Danny if he has seen Doris today?"

The next thing Brenda's mother said was, "Oh, well, I'll get my car and see if I can find her and Danny too. Okay, good-bye."

That was an upsetting day. It took them until evening to locate Doris and Danny. They were laying on blankets in the sun, heads propped up on towels in bathing suits, holding hands. They had made a little lean-to under some big maple trees. Brenda was the one who spotted the lean-to and then they found them.

This episode created some problems that summer. Not only was Doris grounded and not allowed to ride her horse or go to the river or go to the pool in town, Brenda by default did not get to go many places either. Doris refused to do her chores and Brenda and her mother ended up doing a lot of them. Danny was not allowed to call or talk to Doris and his mother spread some unkind rumors around town about Doris.

Doris cried a lot and she was angry at Brenda for finding them. Brenda kept trying to explain to her that they were all worried and they had to find her. Doris wrote more poems, climbed up in the big chestnut tree and did not talk to any of them the rest of the summer.

Brenda's parents had been a bit frantic during that time. Brenda had not acted "boy crazy" as their mother put it and they were very worried that Doris would get herself in some kind of trouble with a boy. Brenda thought they would never let them date boys now. But it did fade away some, until Doris hit high school.

She was "boy crazy" for sure and she had lots of boyfriends. She was not a loose girl, she just liked boys a lot. She was pretty and she liked dances and parties and she lived it up. Brenda was pretty and liked boys too but she never spent as much time as Doris did "chasing boys".

The more Brenda thought about those times she just thought she had nothing more she should share with Laurel and Simon. It just made things worse. She had never shared the stories about Doris' youth with her daughters, so at least they could not blurt it out. Better to just stop thinking about Doris and her children.

As the day went along, she got out the Christmas decorations after all. She would just make a nice Christmas for her and Mike. She was tired of her role as the big sister, protector, and co-conspirator. Now she could just relax and be Brenda with her big heart and her sweet husband.

Laurel

When Simon left for home on the Sunday after Thanksgiving, he and Laurel both agreed that they were okay with all the information they had about their mom. They both just wanted to move on. It had been a weird 6 months and although everything would take a while to settle, neither of them wanted to live in that world of confusion and hurt.

Laurel dialed Brad Collier's phone number and he answered. "Hey! How are you doing?"

Laurel laughed and said, "Oh better than can be expected after a family holiday. I was calling to see if you would like to come for dinner tomorrow night and talk about the things we need to be focusing on to get ready for our spring work."

Brad replied, "Sure, that sounds great. I have been thinking about it a lot and I have some things I want to propose with you. What time shall I get there?"

Laurel said, "5:00! Farmer time! Oh, and Brad, I also just want to see you. I missed you the past few days."

Brad chuckled and said, "Right back at ya Olsen!"

The relationship went into full gear from that day onward. They found each other in the Yakima Valley, both independent, but both of them open to love. It was beautiful.

Simon

When he returned home after Thanksgiving, he decided to write a book. Fiction, based on his mom and he planned to fill in gaps and make it whatever it turned into. It was the perfect time to do it. He was fully employed, he had a great place to live and a view of the water, essential for writing in his mind.

He told Nate his plans and he was very enthusiastic. He thought that Simon had the skill and the sensitivity needed to write. Nate told Selene and she said that it was part of Simon's path and through it he would gain knowledge about himself and his family. It was just waiting to be revealed.

Simon set up a spot in the condo and when

he had moments to spare and sometimes late into the night, he sat facing the bay and crafting his tale of a young woman on a farm.

Simon found himself lost in the novel. He would be talking to friends and desperately want to talk about his characters and where they might be headed. He found that it was a short conversation so he stopped trying. He just immersed himself in the ideas and visions he had about what a young woman like Doris might be thinking. What drove her? He called her Della in the book. He changed many things but the basic struggles were included. It only took him 6 months to write it.

Nate was his editor and agreed it was worthy of publishing. It helped to have personal connections. Not many first novels make it with publishers, but Simon had a skill and lots of exposure to writers. It turned out just the way he thought it would. He wanted to take it home now to Laurel.

So, June 1, 2013, he arranged for two weeks off. He called Laurel to see if he could stay with her at the farm. He promised to help her if she needed it. But she said she and Brad were really making a go of it, both romantically and business wise. She said he could relax at her place, visit Uncle Peter, go see Uncle Mike and Aunt Brenda and anything else he wanted to do.

When he arrived at the farm he was amazed

at how beautiful it looked. The house was re-painted white with dark green trim. The fence around the yard had been replaced with fence made of lodge pole pines, courtesy of Brad's parent's property in Oregon. The old lawn furniture was replaced and a gazebo was being built in the back yard. New wooden screen doors hung on the back and front doors. They were painted green like the trim.

The barn had been cleaned up considerably and there was a counter across the front with a freshly painted sign hanging above it that read "Olson Farm". It had a rail fence, an apple tree and the climbing red roses painted on the sign. It was beautiful. It was a replica of their mom and dad's headstone.

The shed had two new freezers, new shelves, potato and onion bins and stacks of boxes outside of the produce room that were stenciled "Olson Farm Produce".

A lot had happened in the 6 months since Christmas. At Christmas he had visited and that is when he met Brad. It was instant friendship between them. Brad had grown up outside Eugene and he was very at ease with all kinds of people. He knew how much Laurel loved Simon and he could see right away that it was based on Simon's personality. He saw Simon as funny, smart, open to information, and full of love for his sister.

Simon thought that Brad was great. A big farmer, easy to laugh, always looking at Laurel like she was the most beautiful girl in the world, and he was as hard working as his sister.

Christmas was spent eating, drinking, getting Uncle Peter to the house and not going to Uncle Mike and Aunt Doris' house like they often used to do. In fact, on December 26, Laurel asked Simon if he thought it would be nice to see if they would like to come over and have some homemade chili and bread later that week. Simon was happy to do that and he had brought cheese from a creamery in northern Whatcom County that was especially delicious. He volunteered to make the bread. Brad was invited too, but he said he was going to drive to see his family. He also said, "This is a time for just the four of you, I think."

It was the first time any of them had seen each other since the disastrous Thanksgiving dessert affair. Laurel and Simon wanted it to be casual food wise, but they really took care to make everything look beautiful. The table was set with one of their mom's Christmas table clothes. It had holly and pine cones around the edges and was big enough to fit the big table in the kitchen. They used a series of candles and pine cones as the center piece.

Laurel wore a dress she had kept of her mom's. It was green with blue and yellow polka dots. It had a matching belt and she wore her hair up in a nice neat bun and wore a pair of emerald earrings that she bought at an antique shop in Seattle.

Simon wore a pair of black slacks, a crispy white t-shirt and a red V-neck sweater. His hair was in a neat pony tail and Laurel tied a piece of red leather around the length of it in a crisscross pattern. They both looked very fine.

Uncle Mike and Aunt Brenda arrived on time; 4:00 for drinks. When Simon answered the front door, Aunt Brenda broke into tears and he grabbed her into his arms immediately. He whispered, "Please don't cry Auntie. Please, we love you still."

Uncle Mike patted him on the shoulder and said, "Great to see you, Simon."

Laurel came around the corner from the kitchen and soon she was locked in the same embrace with Simon and Aunt Brenda. She turned to Uncle Mike and said, "Whiskey?".

It was a fine evening. Everyone talked about what they had been doing since Thanksgiving. Mostly small talk and some good laughs. The food was delicious and Aunt Brenda asked if she could take home some of the bread and cheese.

They only touched on Thanksgiving and of course it was Simon who said, "Thanksgiving was unfortunate for sure, but you know, Laurel and I are doing fine. I hope you guys are feeling okay too. We are not holding any grudges, but to be honest, our relationships with Angela and Carrie were not strong since we have been adults and that's probably how it will stay. No offense to anyone."

Uncle Mike spoke first as Aunt Brenda was tearing up again. In fact, she was crying off and on all evening. "We are doing fine. It's been hardest on Brenda, but she is seeing a counselor now. The girls do not know about it and it is probably better that way. We see them, but there is still some distrust between us. No problem though. It's just how family can be, right?"

Laurel reached for Brenda's hand and said, "Families are definitely not perfect, but they matter."

That was the extent of the conversation about Thanksgiving. Doris' name never came up except when Brenda recognized the dress that Laurel was wearing. Simon and Laurel did not discuss their mom either and it felt strange, but appropriate. This family was not the type to harp on things and the topic was not open for discussion.

When they left there were many hugs, kisses, and promises to come together soon. Laurel said she would set up a time for lunch after the new year. Uncle Mike said he was planning to go over to Peter's the next day and thought he would haul some garbage that had accumulated.

As their aunt and uncle drove down the driveway leaving the Olson Farm, Simon said, "Dare I say, that puts to rest that shit show at Thanksgiving? It's enough for me."

Laurel nodded in agreement. It felt good to have a great visit with them and it felt good to close the door as they left. Time to move on.

But now it is summer and Simon had just pulled in the driveway. Laurel's pickup was not there, so he got out and stretched and looked at all the improvements. There was a guy there who was painting the gazebo. He was a young- er version of Brad and when Simon introduced himself the painter said, "Oh yeah, Laurel said you would be getting here. I am Brad's nephew, Wyatt. I am working for him and for Laurel too this summer. Nice to meet you."

His hand shake was firm and he looked like he was in his mid-twenties. Simon thought he was probably a college student. He too was tall and well-built and he had a shock of light brown wavy hair that kept falling over his eye. Simon thought he was a very good-looking man.

Simon told him he was going to be staying for a couple of weeks. Simon laughed and said, "You can be guaranteed some summer in the Yakima Valley. Not so much where I live."

"Where's that?"

"In Bellingham, up by the Canadian border. We..."

Wyatt started laughing and said, "Simon, I live there too! I am at WWU, senior year. Wow, so cool!"

Simon smiled a big smile and said, "Do you like it up there?"

Wyatt said, "I freakin' love it! I don't ever want to leave. I grew up in John Day Oregon and it is hot, dry, and red-neck. I could not wait to leave!"

Simon laughed and said, "Same reason I went myself. You can get all of that here in the Yakima Valley; hot, dry, red-neck, and unfriendly to gays."

Wyatt grinned and said, "I am glad you said that. I thought you were, but I didn't want to sound too familiar. Yeah, I am too, so I hear ya. My Dad was the County Sheriff besides so I had to go!"

Simon said he would take his bags in and asked if Wyatt needed a break and a cold drink. "Sounds great," said Wyatt. "I've been painting since 7:00 a.m. and it is time for a cold beer, if that is something you have with you."

Simon smiled and said, "I have beer from our favorite town even."

The two of them sat in some of the new lawn furniture and enjoyed the beauty of Laurel's yard and garden. They shared a joint and discussed clubs, restaurants and favorite hikes in Bellingham. They talked about local music and realized they had been at several of the same venues at the same time.

Simon remarked, "I never expected to meet a kindred spirit this summer. I usually avoid all people I grew up with when I am here and stick to my sister and my Uncle Peter. Have you met Peter yet?"

Wyatt answered quickly. "Yes! I went there the other day with Laurel and helped her clear some vines off his old front porch. Brad thinks they should repair it and I think he has Laurel convinced. I am telling you, when Brad and Laurel decide to do something, it happens. I really admire their work ethic. I can barely keep up with them and Brad is already 40."

"Did you meet Peter?"

"Well, I kind of did. He came out and stood quite a ways away from us. He only spoke with Laurel, well, like two words. I did not take offense though. He is a unique dude for sure."

"That's Uncle Peter," said Simon. "I have really come to appreciate him in the last year. He is honest and what you see is what you get. I find it refreshing."

The conversation lasted for a couple of hours and then Wyatt said, "Shoot, I have got to get back to work. I promised this would be done today. The bosses will be on me if it is not done!" Then he laughed. He laughed a lot and Simon liked it.

Laurel

It was so good to have Simon home. Every day they had breakfast and coffee together. Every night they sat in the yard, drinking and talking. Brad and Wyatt joined them some times and there was a lot of laughter and quite a bit of flirting going on between Wyatt and Simon. It all felt just right.

Laurel told Simon some of her plans for the property. She and Brad were doing some exchanges of fruits and vegetables and still pursuing their own fruit stand operations and farmer's markets. She had expanded the garden by half an acre and she hired her old friend Carla's teenage daughter to help her. Carla had finally divorced her cheating husband and was living in a small house right in town. Her daughter, Beth, was 15 years old and needed a job to afford her school clothes. Laurel was happy to have her working alongside her. She was a good kid, energetic and not sassy.

In fact, Laurel met her when she called Carla after Christmas and asked her to lunch. She did not invite Maria. The two old friends sat in the warm kitchen and Laurel told Carla if she wanted to talk about Lyle and all of that, it would be fine with her. She said, "I don't talk to people about other people here and I am not going to start. There is too much gossip as it is..."

Carla did open up. She had started the process of divorcing Lyle. She had two girls (15 years old and 12 years old) and a little boy who was 10 years old. She said Lyle had used up all that they had and now she was faced with working and trying to make ends meet. Carla's dad had just moved her and the kids into a rental he had in town. She said he did not ask for rent and she said there was no money to give him if had wanted her to pay. Apparently, Lyle's family was in a bit of denial when it came to his problems and they had begged her not to move out. But she said, "I can't continue with this life. It is killing me and my kids."

Laurel asked her what she might be interested in doing for work and she said, "I always wanted to be a florist or work in a greenhouse operation, but I only have a gardener's knowledge, no training of course."

Laurel said, "I have met a lot of nice people since I started this produce business. Someone out there has something for you. I'll call some people. Why don't you talk to Maria's husband Jake? He seems like he knows everyone and he is nice. You will see, a job is waiting for you."

That was the beginning of a revived friendship for the two of them. There were more lunches, dinners with the kids and calls back and forth. Carla did find work and when Laurel said she had to have some help with her garden and harvesting, Beth said, "I can do it!"

Laurel felt good about how her circle was growing slowly and filling with good people that she chose to be around. No more doing what was expected of her. No more pursuing a career she did not like. No more loneliness.

Laurel told Simon she was thinking about using the farm as a wedding venue. All the brides wanted to get married on farms now and she had decided that would be a good way to advertise her farm and get people coming for her future fruit stand on the property. She had her first wedding booked for the year in August. There was a lot to be done, but she was determined to make it work. The wedding was a couple from Yakima she had met at her farmer's market stall. She had created a flyer with Wyatt's help stating Olsen Farm was open for weddings, anniversaries, and other events. They visited and were sold. They would say "I do" in the gazebo.

Simon shared his novel with Laurel and gave her a rough draft copy to read. She read it as she fell asleep at night, so it took a while. She was always so tired at bed time it was hard to stay awake. So far, she thought it was brilliant. His characters came alive, but you did not feel like you were reading their mom's life story. Della was different and very much the same. Without ever having talked to Brenda, he had made her character a little wild and always attracted to handsome men. Someday Brenda would read it and realize she did not need to tell them about that part of her sister's life. Simon just seemed to know it.

When the two weeks were over and Simon was packing to go back, Wyatt pulled in to the yard on his motorcycle and rushed up to Simon and threw his arms around him. They stayed locked in an embrace for minutes and when they pulled apart Laurel could not hear what they were whispering, but she knew they were not done with each other. Bellingham was going to be an even happier place come September for both of them.

Brenda

Brenda was 63 years old now. She was still energetic, but not at her old level. Now she would take her time on a project and try to really enjoy it. She continued to write and unbeknownst to her or Simon, they were both writing about Doris. She too had continued with her fictional version, sprinkling it with so many memories of her sister and their 58 years of life together.

She was still seeing a counselor. She had found a nice woman to go to in Yakima. She had a small counseling business and had one other counselor in her office. When Brenda first went to her, she would cry the entire appointment and most of the way home. Her guilt was almost paralyzing and her sense of loss for her sister and for the relationship with her niece and nephew and daughters was too much at once. She worked through each and every thing she needed to. She fought for some happiness and normalcy. It was a real slog.

By the time summer had arrived she was doing much better. She had started taking an aerobics swimming class at the local pool early in the mornings. It was an indoor pool, bequeathed to the school district by a rich patron. It was called the Carl Jensen Aquatic Center. She met up with some good friends at the pool three days a week and she found it exhilarating. She had always been slim, but she was tightening up her sagging thighs a little.

She would call Laurel most Sundays and check in with her. Laurel was in love with her new life and her new guy. Brenda just wished Doris could have seen this romance. The two of them were made for each other and they came over to Brenda and Mike's for dinner a few times. Brad was just what Laurel needed and vice versa.

She saw Angela and Carrie at least once a week, but not until spring came. She was harboring some intense resentment herself and she and her counselor agreed that space would not break the mother-daughter bond permanently. When she was with them, they were careful to just talk about their children and their lives; no mention of gossip they had heard about Laurel and her new man Brad. Of course, there was gossip and talk about her and Carla becoming close and on and on. All unnecessary but fascinating when your world is a small town.

They never apologized to their mother. They might have regretted it, but chances are they did not. They had spoken their minds and they both meant it. Laurel and Simon were not important to them and they really were not interested in how important they were or weren't to their mother. She was their mother, not the cousin's mother, and there was nothing their cousins could do about it. What they did not realize was that Laurel and Simon still loved their own mom in spite of all the things they were told. She was forever the most important woman in their lives. They had bigger hearts and more open minds than the cousins could have imagined.

When Brenda heard Simon was in town, she called him and asked if she could come over one morning for coffee and cinnamon rolls she planned to bake for him. When she got there, they had a nice conversation. He was happier than she could ever remember. He told her he had been writing and when his book got published, he would send her one. She did not mention her writing. She knew it would pale in comparison to Simon's.

They talked about all that Laurel had done to the farm and both of them were big admirers. It was beautiful and so much more to come. Simon took her on a tour of the produce room and the barn, which was being completely re-done inside with a dance floor, bar, etc. They sat on the benches in the new gazebo and admired the view of the garden and the flower beds.

When Brenda left, she hugged Simon hard and told him she loved him. She said, "You got the very best of your mom and of Diego too. He was such a nice man, so happy and fun. I hated to see him go."

Simon smiled and said, "I think my pen name is going to be Peter Diego, after my Uncle Peter and the Italian who gave me this black hair and long nose!"

As Brenda drove home, she found herself smiling, window down and her hair blowing around her face. She felt younger than she had in a long time.

Doris

Doris was bright, but she was not studious. High school had been fun with all of the socializing, but nothing she had studied really took hold of her. She was not part of the generations to come that would take "gap" years after high school, but it was essentially her plan. It was based on the fact that she had no plans.

Brenda was married already. She met a very nice man when she went to Yakima Valley College right out of high school. She too was not really studious and the college classes were just a blur. But when she met Mike, she just knew he was the man for her.

Doris did not have one man yet. She was dating different boys she knew, but casually. She had not really felt like she was in love since she was 13 years old when she fell for Danny Gordon. After that she liked a lot of boys, but no one made her feel like she wanted to marry them.

Several of her girlfriends were already married. They got married in June, right after graduation. She was in a couple of weddings the summer after high school. She had been the maid of honor at Brenda's, of course.

She attended wedding showers and was fitted for bride's maid's dresses. She worked at the local fruit warehouse during cherry harvest, prune harvest, apricots and that fall in the apples. She put money in the bank and continued to go on dates. But what she really wanted out of life, she just did not know and was a little embarrassed by it.

She felt like everyone she knew had a purpose or passion for something they wanted out of life. For her sister Brenda it was children, a house, a farm. That was just what her husband Mike wanted too, so they had a purpose. Her friends who had married that summer wanted basically the same thing. Two of her high school friends went off to a 4-year college. They had parents who said they would pay the tuition. Mostly they were richer kids and maybe their dad and mom had gone to college. It was just part of what they did in their family.

Doris' parents did not go to college. They both just worked hard. It was what they did. Her mom did not work outside of home and it was expected that she never would. There dad did some farming and he also worked as a part-time accountant for some of the bigger farms. They seemed very happy and they really did not put any pressure on their daughters about the future. When Doris asked her mom what she thought she should do now her mom said, "Well, it seems like you enjoy work and you like having your own money. Maybe, just keep working and see what happens! You will meet someone someday and start a little family, I know that for sure."

She talked to her sister Brenda about what she should do and Brenda said, "Go to Yakima and take some courses. That's where I found Mike and I would never have met him if I didn't go. Plus, maybe you will like college. I did not, but you might."

Doris already thought she was getting old. She turned 19 in August. The thought of turning 20 and not knowing what you were doing sounded horrible. She would still be in her room at home, eating dinner with her parents, borrowing their car to do anything. She started to feel like life might be passing her by.

When Paul started courting her in the fall, she enjoyed it. He was a little old fashioned, but he was still fun. He was a man who loved his mother very much, and Doris' grandma once told her, never marry a man who is mean to his mother. In fact, Doris liked his mother as much as she liked him.

Her name was Gerda and she spoke with a thick Norwegian accent. She was a short and sturdy woman with blonde hair that had turned gray. You could still see streaks of the blonde. She braided it in two long braids and wrapped it around her head. She wore an apron all day. Everything went in the apron pockets and she kept a bag of horehound candy in one of the pockets. She laughed a lot and she was always busy. Doris never saw her sit down unless it was for dinner. She had lost her husband years before and she was used to doing most things around the farm.

She had learned how to cook more American style as her husband and boys never really loved lutefisk or lamb. They were all about the beef and pork, so she adjusted. She did make beautiful breads, cardamom rolls, lefse, and rye tack. She baked cookies that were delicious and used ginger and cinnamon heavily in most of her baking.

She liked Doris. Doris was not a fussy girl. She wore very little make up and usually none at all. She wore her hair long and did not dye it and wore it in a long braid to keep it out of her way. She liked that Doris could cook and understood how to grow flowers and vegetables. Doris could name every flower in the garden and she knew how to can fruits and vegetables.

Gerda told her stories of the old country. Gerda longed for Norway. She spoke of the mountains and the fjords and the green valleys. She missed the moose and the sheep on the mountain sides. She missed her family because she was the only one who came. She had stories of the passage by ship and the people she met who were also coming to America.

She did come with a cousin who was about the same age. They took passage over the Atlantic and then by rail to Seattle. They moved into a Norwegian community in Seattle and got a little apartment. They both found work as nannies. But her cousin got sick with pneumonia and died very suddenly.

That's when Gerda met Paul's father, James. He was looking for a bride. It was not so uncommon in those days to declare that you were looking for a bride. James was planning to move and have a farm and he needed someone to share the load with him and have some children who could work with them too. He was a Lutheran and so was Gerda. It was as close as she could get to the Church of Norway which was the church she grew up attending. James came looking for a bride. She said he took one look at her and asked her to allow him to take her for Sunday dinner. She went and it was not long until she was writing home to let them know that she was getting married. They married at the courthouse in downtown Seattle and then got a train to the Yakima Valley.

Gerda spoke fondly of him and she married him not so much out of love, but because she was so alone and had no one who she could depend on. Her English was still not very good and James needed someone too. He had moved from the mid-west and he too was alone. James turned out to be a good man and they had 8 boys, one right after another.

Gerda appreciated the way Doris listened to her stories. Her own boys never seemed interested and most of them had left the valley behind. She also liked that Doris was especially nice to Peter. Most people just ignored Peter when they realized he was not "all there". But Doris made a point of talking to him just enough to make him comfortable. Gerda thought Peter might love her as much as Paul did.

So, when Paul suggested they get married, Doris thought, why not? He comes from nice people, he works hard, he has a lovely mom, he's buying a house and some land, it's perfect. She did not think I am head over heels in love with this man and I cannot live without him. Instead, she thought, we can have a good life and I will be close to my folks and my sister.

She enjoyed the first years of their marriage. They were very busy fixing up the farm. She put the money she had saved working in the warehouses into the farm too. They planted and painted and scrubbed and planned.

She was happy when she found she was pregnant for the first time. Paul was happy too and Gerda was very excited. She did not have any grandchildren living near her and she longed to hold a little baby.

Of course, Doris' family was happy too. Brenda had two little girls that were 2 and 4 years old. How much fun to have children that could play together and lived nearby. Little did they know that the cousins would someday part ways. Things were good at that time.

Little Laurel was the light of their life. She came out with curly brown hair and light blue eyes. She was pretty as a picture and both of her grandma's were crazy about her. Paul would come in at lunch time and if she was not napping, he would carry her out to the barn to pet the cows and the horses. He would sit her down in the chicken run and laugh while she chased the hens. They were very happy.

Then came the summer when Laurel was 3 years old. It was a hot summer, high 90's and

100 many days. It was going to be a good harvest for all of the crops. Paul was particularly busy that year as he was working with a couple other farmers too. Doris was weeding the garden and flower beds and putting up produce starting in March with the asparagus.

In early May there was a knock on the door one morning and there stood a tall handsome young man. He was dressed a little sharper than the average farmer was and he had the most beautiful thick hair that he had let grown longer than most of the men you saw in the valley at that time. He had it pulled back and tied with a piece of leather. He introduced himself and he had an accent that Doris had never heard before.

He said he was Diego Lombardi and was a student at the University of Washington. He was from Sicily in Italy. He was going to be spending the summer interviewing farmers regarding irrigation and how they utilized it for his dissertation. He was camping on the river in a tent for the summer.

There were instant sparks between them. Doris had never experienced it in her life. He felt it too and when she offered him a glass of lemonade he stepped into her bright and cheerful kitchen and never wanted to leave.

They saw each other every day that summer. Diego did not have a boss for the summer, so he got most of his work done in the early morning and managed to spend afternoons with Doris and her darling little girl Laurel. He helped her with the garden, he admired her flowers and he rode their horse wildly around the pasture. Doris mentioned him to Paul, but she did not mention how much time he was spending there. Paul was so busy this time of year and Diego rode a bicycle everywhere so sometimes Paul did not even know he was there when he drove to the barn on the tractor.

Doris felt like a teenager again. Each time she saw him her heart skipped a beat. When he stole a kiss in the kitchen while Laurel was napping, she did not even think whether it was wrong or right. She turned and kissed him hard and long and she tingled from head to toe. He smelled fantastic, he felt amazing and strong with muscular brown arms. She felt like she was flying when they were locked in an embrace. She felt reckless and vibrant. It was passionate vibrant love. Her first real love and her last as it goes.

The nights of sneaking out became second nature. Paul slept like a rock. Laurel was a good sleeper too and Doris just took the chance she might wake up. Paul would not hear her if she did. It was worth the risk in her mind.

They met in the deep grass in the orchard. Diego always brought a blanket. Their love making was unbridled. Doris had never made love like that to Paul. Paul was not made of the same stuff as Diego.

Concentration slipped away and she found herself staring at the driveway, waiting for his bicycle to appear. Her sister Brenda saw what was happening. She brought her girls over to play with Laurel and she saw her sister in a way she had never seen her before. She glowed from head to toe. She had never been more beautiful and she was considerably beautiful already. Brenda tried to talk to her about it and Doris just laughed and said, "It will be fine. Stop worrying." Brenda worried, but Doris sunk in deeper.

Diego and Doris always knew that the separation they would experience in mid–September would be painful. They talked about it, and Diego could see no future as a couple. Doris told him she would leave Paul and bring Laurel and they would live with him in his tiny apartment at the University. She said she would move to Italy and it did not matter that she might not see her family again. Diego held her close and told her, "You cannot come and live with me. I will not take you away from your home, your family and your husband. I cannot."

Doris cried but Diego would always get her to stop by saying, "Please, my beautiful girl, just enjoy every second we have together. It is all we can ask for."

Doris thought she was prepared for the separation and in her heart, she just knew it would not be forever. How could he really just walk away? She knew he would come back for her or at least write to her and she could go to Seattle to see him. It would all be possible, because of love. Pure and true love.

That was her downfall. When he first left there were tears and even little Laurel cried because her mom was crying. He had only been gone for a few days when the morning sickness arrived. She knew what it felt like from her pregnancy with Laurel. She knew it had to be Diego's. She made sure she had sex with Paul as much as possible after that. This baby would come a little early, but Paul would never know why or even if he suspected, he would never ask.

Doris pulled through those days because she had a baby inside and she did not want to risk the baby's health or her own. She started to caress her belly and murmur words of love that were really for Diego. She imagined this baby looking like Diego and she was ecstatic that she would have a piece of him with her always. She became wrapped up in the dream of having his baby and the idea that someday she would present the baby to him and he would never be able to leave her.

When the baby was born, he had dark hair

and dark eyes. He was a beautiful little boy. Paul named him Simon, an old family name from the Olsen clan. Doris wanted to name him Luca. So, he was named Simon Luca Olsen. Luca was Diego's middle name. When her sister asked her why she chose Luca she said, because it means "bringer of light" and she thought it would be fitting. Brenda answered, "It is also Italian. I understand."

No one but the sister's seemed to realize that Simon was not Paul's baby. Paul, least of all. He carried Simon as soon as he came in the door at night and took him to see his mother and brother as soon as he could get him a little car seat. Laurel adored her brother and kissed and hugged him constantly. Sometimes she declared he was her baby and would tell her Aunt Brenda, "Don't pick up Simon. He wants me to do it." Doris and Brenda thought it was so precious as she was only 3 and could not lift him yet.

Grandma Gerda was suspicious, but she never said anything to Paul. Instead, she confided in Peter, whom she believed would never speak a word of it. Diego had interviewed Gerda and Peter about their farm as part of the irrigation project, so she had met him and he had been very kind to Peter. After Paul would leave the house with little Simon, Gerda would say to Peter, "That is a little Diego." She had no idea how that would carry through Peter's life. He never forgot the kind dark Italian and what his mother said about him.

At first Simon's entry into the family was grand. It actually continued that way until he started to grow into a little boy who was partial to his mom and all things inside and domestic. That was the change that drove Paul crazy.

Doris finally gave up the idea that Diego would ever contact her or return when Simon was about 2 years old. She had been in deep denial about the future. She had lived off of the dream of being with Diego for so long she had convinced herself it could happen. It was in that summer when she first broke apart.

It was not gradual as one might expect. Instead, it came on quickly and for both Doris and Paul it was a shock. One morning she was washing up the breakfast dishes and she looked out the window and it hit her. She had unconsciously been looking for Diego's bicycle for two years. She crumpled onto the floor and sobbed. She kept saying out loud, "I have wasted myself. I am nothing now. I am nothing."

Little Laurel had grabbed Simon's hand and ran to the barn screaming for her dad. He was right there and he grabbed them both up and Laurel said, "Mama is on the floor crying. She won't get up, Daddy."

The first time Paul waited a few days before

he realized he could not help her. She could not stop crying for most of the day. She did not want to do anything. She curled up in a ball on their bed and refused food. Paul was frantic. That was the first trip to the 5th floor. There were more to come.

After three visits to the psych ward, Doris finally recovered enough to carry on with her normal life. She went through grief, but she also had a lot to do and two darling little ones to take care of. Mostly she worked hard and kept it all locked down inside of her.

One day when she went to take the children to see Gerda and Peter, Gerda handed her a cup of coffee and asked her to sit down and visit with her. Peter followed the children outside, as he liked to do, so he could watch them playing. Gerda patted Doris' hand and said, "You have had true love in your life. Some never know it. I never did. Little Simon Luca will always be the face of that love."

Doris grabbed Gerda's hand and said in Norwegian, "Jeg elsker deg." That translates to I love you.

No more was ever spoken again. Doris kept that treasure in her heart for the rest of her life. She did truly love Gerda.

Doris In the End

The swelling in her stomach had been no-
ticeable for several months. Doris had
never been heavy, but she also had never
been 58. At first, she thought it was a weight
gain and she tried to cut back on eating, but
she realized, she was not a big eater to begin
with, so off to the doctor.

She never bothered Paul with health issues.
She felt a tremendous amount of guilt for the
money she had cost him when she went in
and out of the hospital. She held back some of
her inheritance and she asked Brenda to open
an account for her under Brenda's name and
that is the money she always used for doctor
bills. It was another secret, but she felt that

was no longer something she felt guilty about; she kept secrets.

Brenda went with her to the doctor appointment. The next week she went back for tests and scans and then a biopsy. They told her it was inoperable pancreatic cancer. Once she heard about the treatments and the few months it might extend her life, she decided this was something no one but Brenda was going to know about.

The cancer felt like it was a comeuppance for the lie that she told Paul and everyone else. She felt like this was the punishment and she decided that no one else was going to suffer because of it. No one but Brenda, but Brenda had been the truest and best sister in the world and she knew she could ask her to do this for her.

Brenda would not hear of this decision. She was upset and said a lot of things about fighting for your life and staying as long as you can for family and saying good-bye properly and on and on. Doris could hear her, but she was not at all persuaded. In fact, she had often thought that if she ever was diagnosed with cancer that she would not take treatment.

She had been there for poor Gerda as she died a painful death from colon cancer. It was months of treatments with painful side effects. As she loss control of her body, Doris took care of her as much as she could with two small children. Again, Brenda stepped in and helped her with Laurel and Simon.

But Paul, he just disappeared inside himself. He stayed away from his mother, who cried for him and begged Doris to bring him to see her. He said he could not bear to see her like that. Doris tried to tell him that his mother was the one suffering and he had to bear it because she was bearing it. Paul was frozen. He would not go see her.

Peter was with her every day and when they brought in hospice, he and Doris stayed with her all of the time. Paul helped with the children and kept working. A couple of the sons who had left long ago returned to say goodbye. Doris met sisters-in-law she had never seen and brothers she had only heard of in family stories. For the last month there was someone almost every day.

Doris watched and wished they could have come more often when Gerda felt strong and was happy and would have loved to cook for them. But they waited and came when she could not even respond anymore. It had a huge impact on Doris.

She thought about Paul and how he had always been beside his mother for all of his life. She wanted him there now, but she knew he gave his mother so much joy when she could really experience it. It made his decision a little easier for Doris.

Watching Gerda's passing left Doris with a strong conviction that no matter when or what cancer got her, she would go on her own terms. So, when she told Brenda what she was planning to do, there was no talking her out of it. In fact, she refused to discuss it further.

She found the way to get the medicine and to protect Brenda. She never told her that it was through a drug dealer that she found out about from a farm hand on the neighboring farm. She kept it all to herself, but she did ask Brenda's help in setting up the funeral arrangements and picking the head stone. Brenda begged her to tell Paul and the kids, but she said absolutely not. "Maybe they will know some day, but I am not putting any of them through a long slow painful death."

Doris did not want to die. She did not want to leave her family and her farm and all the plants and flowers she loved. She did not want to leave Paul and she worried how he would manage without her. She had a feeling about Laurel coming to help him. She just knew Laurel so well and she knew Laurel was loyal to Paul and loved the farm.

She never wanted to say good-bye to Simon. He was the product of her true love and he was all the things she loved about Diego. Of all the family that she might tell, it would have been Simon. She wanted to tell him how wonderful his father had been and that even though he left her, he was doing the best thing for her and for Paul and for Laurel. He was a good Catholic and he did not believe in divorce, truly, and he would not have wanted her to leave her family. They just fell in love and he did not take advantage of her. She was a willing partner through it all.

But, as you know dear reader, she did not tell Simon. She did not tell anyone and she left on her own terms. She left suddenly, but sometimes sudden death is easier than prolonged death. The grief is immediate. The loved ones left behind did not spend months of agony, wishing that they could stop the suffering of the person who was so sick. Slow death was like pulling off a band aid slowly. Ripping off a band aid hurts, but it ends.

She left with no regrets about taking her life. She left at peace with it all. She believed in the afterlife and she believed she would be forgiven for all the things she had done. She knew that she would meet with those who left before her and she had no worries about what would happen to her after death. She believed she would be at peace and that love is the only constant in this world and the next. Doris was ready to go.

When Paul left that morning, she told him

she felt a little dizzy and was going to lay back down. She swallowed the pills and she laid down on her freshly made bed. Right before she started to lose consciousness, she thought maybe she should be in the bathroom, in case she had lose bowels or some kind of mess that Paul would need to clean up. When she stood up, she went down and she was gone. That is why she was on the floor when he found her.

Just as she predicted, Paul called the mortuary. He had her embalmed. He was grief stricken, but he did not have to take care of her and watch her fade away into someone he could recognize. She gave him this final gift from her heart and from her deep love for him, the man she called her husband.

THE END

Gwen Delp lives in Bellingham, Washington with her husband, Joe. This is her fifth novel. She grew up in farm country in the Yakima Valley and it is reflected in her work. She retired from a career in social work and administration of public assistance programs. Moving to Bellingham was a life long dream, as well as living in her 1918 home. She continues to write and is working on her sixth novel at the time of his publication.